Town of Ghosts

Olivia Braun

Published by Trellis Publishing, 2021.

TOWN OF GHOSTS

First edition. July 15, 2021.

Copyright © 2021 Olivia Braun.

ISBN: 979-8224597444

Written by Olivia Braun.

TOWN OF GHOSTS

OLIVIA BRAUN

The world felt as if it was closing in on the car as Daniel steered them through icy forest roads. Rachel watched as the light snow and fog got thicker and thicker as they ascended. She wasn't worried. She didn't worry about much anymore. And she didn't miss the view. Her body was on its way to her parents' lakeside cabin on December twentieth - very much against their advice - but her mind was trapped six months in the past, in her home in the small town of Lovelock, Nevada, as it had been ever since her daughter was found face-down and motionless in the bathtub.

"This is a good idea," Daniel said. He wiped dirt off the inside of his glasses with his finger, trying to keep his eyes on the road which was lined either side with enormous, snow-blanketed fir trees. "We've got more than enough supplies to last us a month if we get stuck up here."

It was a terrible idea, Rachel thought. But she let him think that he was helping. She didn't care where she was, truthfully, and was under no illusions that the untimely death of her five-year-old daughter would upset her less after a change of scenery. At least it would save them a little money on rent, she thought. Since Kayleigh died, they hadn't been able to sleep in their house. Money was tight before, but even with a loan from her parents, they were about to hit real trouble.

"There's something up ahead," Daniel said. "This is it, right?"

Rachel sat up a little and squinted. She could make out the shape of it through the fog. It was a two-storey cabin with shutters over the small windows, an old swing-chair hanging on the porch and a wooden deer sculpture out front. The roof was covered with a thick layer of snow and the wooden deer was up to his knees in it. It was only three in the afternoon, but between the snow storm and the fog, it was already getting dark. The car's headlights struggled to pick out the cabin through the snow as they got nearer. The cabin took on more features and color as they drove into the fog. The car, a Toyota four-by-four, pushed through the snow and came to a stop with its lights shining through the windows of the cabin. Rachel hadn't seen the place since she was a teenager.

"It hasn't changed a bit," she said, feeling almost disappointed. "I thought it would look different now, but it's exactly how I remember it."

Daniel left the engine running so they could enjoy the heaters for a few precious minutes before heading outside. Rachel sat and let her mind wander to when she was fifteen, without a care in the world, chasing her sister around the forest with a water gun. Rachel missed her sister terribly. She didn't really miss the person her sister had become, the high-flying attorney who had packed up her husband and three kids for Australia five years ago. She missed the girl she had shared her childhood with, rather than the adult who poked her here and there with phone calls from the other side of the world. Rachel missed the girl that she once was, too, and the world she once lived in.

Rachel started a little when Daniel took her hand.

"It can be like it was," he said. "You just need some time away. You've been doing too much. You need to relax."

Rachel said nothing.

She wasn't convinced.

The cabin looked the same, but inside it was emptier, darker.

Just like me, Rachel thought.

*

Rachel kneeled over the fire and prodded it to get it going, her icy breath floating in front of her face, as Daniel was out back gassing up the generator. The fire was slowly coming alive and filling the musty room with a warm, unsteady glow and Rachel looked around. The bare floorboards were freezing under her knees and the floor, as with everything from what she could make out, was covered with a light coating of dust. The lounge was spacious and furnished with floral-patterned furniture that would have been considered luxurious in the eighties. Rachel had considered it luxurious in the eighties. The bookshelf, her father's favorite hideaway on their summer vacations, was still stocked with reserve copies of everything he had at home. There were psychology reference books, reports and a smattering of fiction - DeLillo and Ballard, mostly - which, as a child, she'd found incomprehensible. In the bottom corner of the bookshelf was a small pile of C.S. Lewis and J.R.R. Tolkien he had bought for Rachel and her sister to keep them quiet, to lessen the more destructive or noisy games that disturbed his reading.

Something moved in the top corner of the room, beyond the bookshelf. Rachel stood and grabbed a duster from the box on the floor. It was a cobweb, dangling from side to side. Wiping it away, she hoped that didn't mean spiders. It had been cold enough up here now that they should've all died out, she told herself.

French doors at the back of the room, past a small dining table, looked out onto a long stretch of snow with a small, now-bare apple tree protruding from it, like a black, skeletal hand reaching up from the earth itself. Rachel tried not to look at it. The tree had always unnerved her as a child. She could hear it rustling in the night as she lay awake in her bed trying to pretend she was safe and sound in Nevada. Past the tree was only a wall of shifting whiteness. The fog and the snow obscured completely Jackson Lake which lay beyond.

Rachel stood and watched the ebb and tide of the whiteness which surrounded the cabin and created for her and Daniel a physical barrier between them and the rest of the world. She was grateful for it - and she was sure her parents were grateful for it, having of late become visibly impatient with her relentless grief - but it also filled her with something approaching dread. She had spent the last six months in an unending fit of despair, one which she wasn't sure she would ever see the other side of. There had been nights when she had convinced herself that her life was over, that it was only a matter of moments before she found the courage to take her own life. But she was still here. She was functioning.

She wasn't entertaining those kinds of thoughts anymore. Entering this void of whiteness, a hole in the weather in which she and Daniel could bury themselves, it felt like hiding. It felt like they were tunneling a safe-house for themselves, deep and far from the rest of the world. Rachel was scared that it would take a considerable effort to pull herself out of this tunnel, and worried that she wouldn't have the strength or the will to do it. They had taken themselves out of the world, essentially, and she didn't know if she would want to go back.

The front door slammed shut and startled her out of her gloomy daydream. She took a breath and rubbed the back of her neck.

"Did you get it going?" she said. "The lights are still off."

She turned and peered into the darkness of the hallway through the open lounge door.

"Dan?" she said.

She heard him kicking the wall to knock the snow off his shoes, but it was too dark to see him with only the small fire to light the place. She walked over to the door.

"Did you find my dad's gas store?" she said. "He said there should be enough there to keep us in as much electricity as we can eat for a few months if it comes to it."

She heard him walked up the stairs, but he didn't speak. Frowning, Rachel walked into the dark hallway.

"Dan?" she said, looking up the stairs. "Where are you going?"

She saw a shadow turn the corner at the top of the stairs as she peered up from the bottom.

"You're not going to help me with these freakin' boxes?"

The silence made her uneasy.

What the hell is his problem? she thought.

"Daniel," she called up. "What are you doing?"

There was no response. She held onto the railing, thinking about following him up into the dark upper floor. Something about him being in the dark up there in silence made her stomach turn. He had been distraught about Kayleigh's death, too, but he had recovered. He had been strong for Rachel. His grief was the quiet kind, the detached kind, not like Rachel's, wailing, dribbling and hitting herself periodically for months on end. Rachel's grief was ugly, she knew that. But never for a moment had Daniel been anything less than her own personal therapist and cheerleader. She couldn't ask any more of him. His silence now was getting to her.

"Daniel," she called up again.

She took a few deep breaths and took the first step up the stairs.

Something screeched outside and the cabin was suddenly filled with harsh, white light. Rachel covered her eyes and curled up. Her heart dropped in her chest and she was overcome with panic.

She heard the front door slam behind her and she turned quickly around.

Daniel was stood in the doorway with a grin on his face.

"I got it..." he started, but the panic on Rachel's face stopped him in his tracks. "What's wrong, Rach?" he said.

Rachel looked up the stairs. The upper floor looked empty. She didn't speak for a moment, listening for movement.

"What is it?" Daniel said. He kicked the snow off his shoes and moved to embrace Rachel.

Rachel put up a hand and said, "Were you just in here?"

Daniel looked confused. "What? No," he said. "I was getting the generator going." He pointed to the working lights and said, "See?"

"I thought I heard you come in," Rachel said.

She looked up the stairs. Daniel's face hardened. He looked up the stairs, too.

"Stay here," he said.

"Wait," Rachel said, reaching out after him as he walked quickly up the stairs, his boots knocking hard on the wooden slats.

He reached the top of the stairs and looked around. Rachel waited with bated breath. He walked away from the top of the stairs and

Rachel listened to his boots on the floorboards. She heard him opening doors, entering rooms, walking around. Rachel put her hand through her hair and tried to calm herself. She leaned against the wall. Something cold and wet made her move her hand away. It was water. She looked at the wall and saw in a faint outline, half destroyed by her touching it, the wet outline of a small hand on the yellow-beige floral wallpaper.

She took a step back and brought her hand to her mouth. Tears hit her eyes and her lungs locked down and stopped her breath.

It was a child's hand-print, still wet.

It was still dripping down the wall, and after a few seconds, it had become a shapeless, watery mark.

The sound of Daniel's footsteps grew louder and he appeared at the top of the stairs.

"There's no-one up here," he said, walking back down. "You sure you heard something?"

Rachel looked at him with tears in her eyes. She swallowed hard and glanced at him to the now-unrecognizable wet spot on the wall.

"What's wrong?" he said, embracing her.

She let herself get lost in his arms and closed her eyes. She started to breathe again.

You're being a freakin' idiot, she told herself. You've lost it. Get yourself together, woman.

"What is it?" he said. "Is it this place? I know it's a little spooky in the dark with the storm and all, but we'll make it cozy, you'll see." He moved back and took her face in his cold hands and looked at her with concern. "Are you OK?" he said.

Rachel dried her eyes and nodded. She attempted a smile. "I just got a little spooked, I guess," she said. "I'm sorry. I'm being childish."

Daniel hugged her close.

"I love you," Rachel said.

"More than anything," Daniel replied, as was their routine.

*

The first night was passing slowly. Rachel and Daniel lay in bed facing in opposite directions, not touching, not speaking, waiting to fall asleep, just like they had done every other night in recent memory. When they were awake and walking around in the daylight, Rachel had moments where she felt things were almost as they were before. She could never pretend Kayleigh was just in the next room - the constant and intense longing in her gut would never go away - but things between her and Daniel at times could be described as normal. He could be charming and loving and kind. He couldn't be funny again yet, even though he'd started trying recently. But when the sun went down and they lay in bed together with nothing but their thoughts, Rachel could hardly bring herself to say his name or look him in the eye. Maybe he felt the same way.

But I wasn't the one who let her drown, Rachel thought.

She closed the thought down almost as soon as she had it. It wasn't healthy, she knew that. It wasn't anyone's fault, that's what she kept telling herself. But, deep down, there was a dark place inside her reserved for such thoughts.

It had been Daniel's turn to give Kayleigh a bath. Rachel could hear her laughing and playing for a while. He was telling her a story about a friendly monster. Rachel fell asleep with a book in her hands. When it dropped from her grasp and hit the floor, it woke her up. There was no laughter to be heard, then. The silence made her feel sick to her stomach, before she'd even known what had happened. When she walked into the bathroom, Kayleigh was face-down in the water. She'd slipped and bumped her head, that's what they said. She was unconscious as the water filled her little lungs. Rachel didn't know what happened after that. She has flashes of memory here and there, of blue lips and cold hands, but nothing substantial to hold onto. She didn't know where Daniel was. She didn't know what she did. She woke up in the hospital. Daniel said he had just stepped away for two minutes, that she was safe when he left her.

But she wasn't safe.

If she was safe, Rachel thought, she wouldn't have drowned.

Rachel lay on her side in bed. The moon was reflecting off the snow outside and it gave the room a light glow. Rachel's eyes were wide open. She was tired, but she couldn't sleep. All she could do, as on any other night, was lay there and think, if she was safe then she wouldn't have drowned.

Rachel slipped the covers off her and wrapped a bathrobe around her on top of her pajamas. She kicked on her slippers and walked downstairs in search of a hot drink.

The light in the kitchen blinded Rachel when she flipped it on. She covered her eyes and stood still for a moment to let her tired eyes adjust. She started making herself a cup of cocoa and she studied her reflection in the night-blackened windows. She had bags under her eyes and her long, auburn hair was a tangled mess. She looked at herself long enough to realize that she couldn't see anything on the outside. The windows were open to the outside world but acted only as dark mirrors for those inside. The thought made Rachel's blood run cold.

Rachel's feet ran cold too. Turning, she saw that the back door had come open slightly and was drifting ever more open with the breeze. The snow storm had calmed, thankfully, but it was still freezing outside. Rachel pushed the door closed gently so as to not wake Daniel. She looked at the cuckoo clock on the wall. It was three in the morning. Rachel stirred her cocoa and took the kettle off the stove. When she flipped off the light switch, she saw a straight line of moonlight coming from behind her.

The back door was ajar again.

Nothing to worry about, Rachel said. I just didn't close it tightly, that's all. That's all it is.

Rachel placed her cocoa down on the kitchen table and walked across the tiled floor to the back door, her slippers scraping as she dragged her feet. Touching the handle of the door, she looked out. Now that it was dark inside, she could see outside.

There was nothing there, just snow and moonlight and the big black hand that was the dead apple tree.

Rachel pushed the door closed gently until it clicked. She took the key from off a hook on the wall to lock it shut. She pressed the key into the lock, but it was stiff. Jangling it, it still wouldn't go.

"Come on," Rachel whispered.

She crouched down and looked inside the keyhole. It was dark. There didn't seem to be anything blocking the way. She took the large key and guided it in with both hands, making completely sure not to twitch or tremble. She didn't want it to go off course. Once the key was in firmly, completely, she turned it slowly and with a small clunk it was locked.

"That wasn't so hard, was it?" she said to herself.

Standing up, she saw a small, pale face peering up from the bottom of the back door window.

Rachel recoiled and fell onto her back, knocking the wind out of herself.

She looked up at the back door window and the face peered over the bottom frame at her with large black eyes. Rachel tried to scream, but her breath hadn't come back. She fumbled around behind her for the light switch. The back door handle was being turned from outside, rattled.

Rachel spun around, flipped the kitchen light on and turned back to the door.

The face was gone.

Rachel caught her breath and didn't blink.

In the light, she could see now the window pane had misted up under where the face had been, under where its breath had come into contact with the glass. Something was written in the condensation, a word smudged into the moisture with a small finger.

Rachel took a tentative step forward to read what it said.

It said: D A D D Y

*

By the time her screaming had woken Daniel and he'd gotten downstairs, the word had faded on the glass.

"I saw someone," Rachel said, pointing from where she sat on the floor with her knees tucked up to her chest. "It was a little kid, I think. There at the back door. Looking in."

Daniel kneeled on the floor beside her and held her. "There's no-one out here, honey," he said. "We're in the middle of nowhere. There's no one else for miles around. It's OK, hush now."

"I saw it," she said.

Daniel kissed her on the forehead and looked her in the eyes as if searching for the truth in there.

"I saw it," she repeated.

Daniel and Rachel didn't sleep for the rest of the night. Daniel stayed up until dawn with her. Neither spoke, but rather sat and read on opposite sides of the room. Daniel was comforting when he spoke, but the fact that he rarely spoke belied his real feelings. He looked almost angry, Rachel thought. There was a tension there, just under the surface. He smiled a little too easily, spoke a little too calmly. Dawn came at long last and with it, Rachel and Daniel prepared breakfast and planned their day. In the light of day, Rachel's fears about the place died away. She walked out to the lake through the back door and didn't give the dead apple tree a second glance. She didn't look for strangers or jump at animal sounds. She simply walked to the lake to see if it had changed.

Jackson Lake sat in the shadow of the magnificent Teton mountains. In the icy weather, they looked like death incarnate, promising only starvation and frost-bite and a painful end in grand isolation. The lake was sealed with a thin sheet of ice which twinkled in the sunlight and the surrounding forests were white with their trees bent and misshapen from the weight of the snow.

Rachel dug in the snow for a moment and dug up a large stone. Walking to the edge of the lake, she threw the stone and listened to it crack through the ice further in and splash as it sank into the depths of the lake.

She stood for a moment and enjoyed the silence. She took a baby step forward and let the water that was coming out from under the cracked ice at the edge touch the bottom of her boots. The cold was creeping through her wool gloves and she started to feel a slow pain coming on, the raw stinging of the water from the snow seeping onto her skin. Rachel thought about how it would feel if that was all over her body, how bad the pain would be and how long it would last if she threw herself into the lake.

The wind rushed through the nearby trees and Rachel closed her eyes and listened to the sound of the branches scraping up against one another. In the noise, she thought she heard words, faint, masked by the wind, or perhaps made from it.

"Dee-add," came the whisper. "Deeeeee-add."

Rachel closed her eyes tighter and listened hard. It was like someone was whispering on the wind, only not quite. It didn't sound like a person.

"Deeee-ad," it came clear as day.

Rachel opened her eyes. She heard it.

"Daddy," it whispered.

Suddenly, a hand touched her back. Rachel leaped around and swore.

"Daniel!" she said.

"Christ," he said. "I'm sorry. I called you. I thought you knew I was here."

He put his arms around her waist from behind and she faced the lake. She was tense. She looked around to see if anyone else was lurking.

I must be going crazy, she thought.

"What are you doing out here anyway?" he said.

"I was just looking," Rachel said, trying not to sound too scared.

"It's a beautiful place," Daniel said. "It could use a little sunshine, but it's real nice up here, don't you think?"

Daniel was holding her tight. A little too tight, Rachel thought.

"I could live up here, I think," Daniel said. "No crowds, no traffic, no noise, just us and mother nature."

Rachel turned in his arms and faced him. She tried to smile.

"You're right," Daniel said. "No internet. We'd hate it."

Daniel smiled, but there was something behind the smile. Rachel didn't know what it was. She'd never seen it before. It unnerved her. It was, again, as if his smile was too genuine, too easy. She used to be able to read him like an open book. Lately, for the past year or so, he'd constructed a wall. Rachel had no idea what went on in his head.

"We better head inside," Rachel said. "Looks like that storm's coming back."

Daniel didn't move. He just looked at her, thinking.

"Daniel?" she said.

He nodded and snapped out of whatever it was that had hold of his attention. "Let's go in," he said. "You're right. Let's batten down the hatches and make that fire earn its keep." He laughed as he took her hand and they walked away from the shore of the lake. His laugh unsettled Rachel, but she didn't know why.

*

Rachel waited impatiently for the night to come. She and Daniel sat by the fire and read, talking very little. She read her dog-eared C.S. Lewis while he poured over her father's textbooks. She wanted to be rid of Daniel and his odd stares and long silences. She wanted to go back out to the lake. Whatever it is, she thought, it's out there. And it's trying to talk to me.

Craziness be damned, she thought. If I'm crazy, I'm crazy, but I have to see.

There was a small part of her that hoped beyond all hope that maybe, just maybe, it was Kayleigh. Rachel had never put much faith in the supernatural or religion, but she had always held out a little bit of hope that there was something else, after all this. Now, having lost the light of her life, she had more hope than ever.

But why would Kayleigh come to her now, after all this time? And why here?

"I think I'm going to head up to bed," Daniel said, yawning and snapping his book closed. "Are you coming?"

Rachel tried to look calm. She smiled as warmly as she could manage. "I'm gonna stay up for a bit longer," she said. "I want to read some more."

"Trapped in Narnia," Daniel said as he kissed her on the top of her head. "Don't stay up too long, hey? I'm just upstairs if you need anything."

"OK," Rachel said.

The next wait was the longest of all. Rachel timed herself. She would wait two hours before going outside. Daniel was sure to be asleep by then. She tried to distract herself with the book, but while her eyes did move over the words none of them entered her mind. Her thoughts were racing. She felt nauseous with worry about herself, about her mental health.

This is how it starts, she thought. It seems a little weird, but you accept it. Then it gets weirder and weirder and you accept it easier and easier until one day you're dressed all in white and lining up for pills in your ward in the nut house.

The clock in the lounge was a smiling Felix the cat. His whiskers were the hands. Rachel had begged her dad to buy that clock one summer when she was a girl. It had taken three whole days to persuade him, and just as long again to persuade him to put it up in the lounge. Rachel stared at Felix until his face was burned onto the back of her eyeballs. His whiskers moved painfully slowly, tick tick ticking along.

Rachel must have dozed off, because after a long blink, it was time. It was three in the morning. Daniel had been upstairs for four hours. There's no way he's awake, Rachel thought.

She pulled on her big winter coat with the fur hood, slipped into her boots, and walked into the kitchen. She turned off the kitchen light before she moved to the back door. It looked lonely outside. It was only in the dark that the isolation of the place really hit Rachel. They were hundreds and hundreds of miles from anyone. Daniel said he hoped she could rest easier, but, if anything, it was making things worse.

Here I am, she thought, walking out into a snow storm at three in the morning looking for ghosts. I have absolutely cracked up.

She opened the door slowly and silently. The snow had piled up a little at the door, the wind having blown it against the house. Rachel looked around with her icy breath hanging in front of her face. She looked beyond the black hand of the apple tree, to the forest beyond, and she squinted to try to see through the light but constant and swirling snowfall to Jackson Lake, but she couldn't. Rachel stepped outside and closed the door, listening for the click of the catch.

The moon was full and bright and the snow-covered ground glowed in its rays. Dark spots in the snow caught Rachel's eye. There were two of them, right in front of her. Rachel covered her eyes with her gloved hands and looked down.

Her heart almost stopped.

Footprints.

It was a pair of child's footprints.

No bigger or smaller than Kayleigh's were, Rachel thought.

She took a deep breath and took a step forward in the direction of the lake, where the footprints were pointing. And as she stepped another set of footprints appeared in front of her. She kept walking, and step after step revealed child's footsteps in front of her. She was being led.

Looking up, peering through the snow, Rachel caught a glimpse of a child running away, its arms flapping by its sides as it ran as fast as it could. It looked back over its shoulder.

It was Kayleigh.

Rachel stopped and dropped to her knees. She was overcome with joy, just seeing her daughter's face.

Kayleigh looked scared.

"Daddy!" Rachel heard her call.

Rachel stood and ran as fast as she could through the snow. The storm was beginning to calm and the half-frozen lake appeared in front of her out of the fog. Kayleigh was gone, but her footprints led to the water. Rachel looked around, panicked.

"Kayleigh," she said. "Kayleigh, please."

"Daddy," a whisper came behind her.

Rachel spun around and was facing the cabin. No-one was stood behind her, but as the storm subsided and the fog drifted away, Rachel could see the cabin clearly. In the bedroom window, Daniel stood watching her.

"Daniel?" Rachel said.

He was fully dressed in his coat, hat, and gloves. He was completely motionless, utterly expressionless. His eyes were locked on Rachel. In the glow of the moon, his face was totally white, and his eyes were deep in shadow. He stared down at Rachel with something that looked like contempt. She had never seen any expression even resembling it on his face before.

He looked like he hated her.

He's been waiting up this whole time, Rachel suddenly thought. But why?

"Daddy," came the voice behind her.

Rachel turned and suddenly, there was Kayleigh, stood with her feet in the icy water of the lake.

"Daddy," she said.

"Baby," Rachel said. She reached out to touch her but stopped just short from fear of making her leave.

"Daddy," she said again.

Rachel started to lose all feeling in her body, starting with her hands. They tingled and then went dead. A feeling of horror swept over her as she started to lose all control of herself as if possessed. Her hands moved forwards of their own accord.

"Wait," Rachel said. "No."

Her hands grabbed hold of Kayleigh, holding her by her shoulders. Rachel fought it with every fiber of her being, but she wasn't in control.

"Daddy," Kayleigh said, "what are you doing?"

Rachel heard her own voice say, "Hush, baby. This won't hurt."

Rachel pushed Kayleigh down in the water. She didn't fight. She smiled, thinking they were playing a game.

"Daddy," she said again, "what-"

Her head was pushed under the water. She barely struggled. Rachel's hands held her there. Kayleigh hardly moved. She trusted it was a game, right until the moment before she passed out when there was a small flash of panic and a muffled scream. And then she was drowned.

"No," Rachel said. "No, no, no."

Her hands wouldn't move. They held Kayleigh's lifeless body down in the icy water.

"Let me go!" she screamed, and suddenly her hands were released.

Rachel fell backward into the snow, screaming and crying. It was him, she thought. He did it on purpose! He drowned her! He drowned her with his own hands! That's what she wanted to show me!

"Rachel," the voice came from behind her.

She turned and stood. He offered his hand, but she didn't take it.

"What are you doing out here?" he said.

Rachel sniffed back her tears.

"I, uh, couldn't sleep," he said. "And I saw you thrashing around out here. You're worrying me, honey."

Rachel couldn't find the words to speak.

"You're worrying everyone," he said. "They don't know what you might do to yourself."

That was it, she thought. That was why now, why here. He'd brought her out here to kill her, to make it look like she'd finally had enough and taken her own life. It was a warning. "Daddy," she said. She was warning her.

"Rachel," he said, "I'm talking to you."

"Stay away from me," she whispered. "I know what you are."

Confused, he nearly laughed. "Rachel, I don't know what you mean. What am I?"

"I know what you did," she said.

His half-smile dropped. He became serious. "What did I do?" he said.

Rachel took a step back and looked behind her. She was on the edge of the lake, her boots in the water.

"It's so quiet up here, isn't it?" he said, taking a step towards her. "You could get away with anything up here."

"Why did you do it?" Rachel said, bursting into tears. Then, screaming, she said, "You drowned her! Why?!"

"I don't know!" he shouted back, leaning towards her. "You don't have reasons for things like this!"

Rachel looked at him, stunned.

"I was going to kill us all," he said, quieter. "I can't take this world anymore. I was going to kill us all, so we could be together. We could finally be as happy as we deserve to be."

Rachel broke down in tears and said, "Kayleigh was happy!"

Daniel wiped tears away from his own eyes and stepped towards Rachel.

"Stay away!" she screamed.

Daniel grabbed her arm with one hand and with the other took out a hunting knife from a sheath under his coat. "Nobody will understand," he said. "Nobody really cares anyway. We're better off this way."

"No!" Rachel screamed. "You're fucking insane!"

She punched and kicked at Daniel, splashing in the water, but he held her still and brought the knife against her chest, the point over her heart. "Hush, baby," he said. "This won't hurt."

A small voice came from behind Daniel. "Daddy," it said.

Daniel turned, and in that moment Rachel grabbed his knife, twisted it back and plunged it deep into his stomach. He screamed for his life and fell to his knees. Rachel stepped away, leaving the knife inside him, as he dropped onto his hands and knees in the water, turning back towards the cabin. In front of him stood Kayleigh. The icy water turned red around him as he looked at his dead daughter in utter terror.

Rachel moved to the shore and watched as he shook his head. "No," he said. He looked at Rachel and said, "Come with me. Be with us." Blood spilled out of his mouth and he collapsed face down in the water.

"You're going to a different place," Rachel said.

Daniel's body went limp in the water. Rachel heard his dying breath, a long final exhalation. And he was gone.

"Mummy," a voice came, and with that Kayleigh vanished into a flurry of snow carried on the wind.

The storm was coming back. The clouds were drawing in overhead, shutting out the moonlight. The world was getting darker, but Rachel felt herself straightening up, the fog of grief lifting from her mind.

She trudged back through the snow as it got heavier and heavier. Slamming the back door behind her, she felt entirely closed off from everyone. The cabin was consumed by the storm. Rachel sat on the kitchen floor with her back to the wall. And though she started to cry, she was filled with this unshakable feeling the likes of which she hadn't felt for years, not since the day Kayleigh was born. Rachel felt that even if the storm worsened, she would be able to survive it.

She could survive anything.

The End.

DARK PORTRAITS

EMILY FORTUNE

Chapter 1

"Wake up Tim, you're as home as you'll ever be."

Tim Morro blinked cautiously out of a sweaty stupor from his side of the cab of a working man's pickup that smelled of farm and oil and Tim's own farts. The brakes complained and the wheels turned against the cracking curb of an unfinished suburb of another, only slightly less desperate suburb of Modesto County, California, fully 50 miles from where Tim had just passed an unproductive night, earning nothing but a heat rash and another in a long list of life's lessons.

And now it was morning, the kind of blurry, sunny, summer California morning that always made Tim wish he was a bat.

"That your dump, isn't it?" The truck belonged to Tito, probably, the Mexican hustler who occasionally found work for Tim as one of many day-laborers who composed Tito's visionary enterprise of making money off the backs of others.

Tim sat fully up and confirmed that this was, indeed, his dump.

"You got anything for me, Tito?"

Tito shook his head, his eyes shut in studious mourning. "Afraid not, amigo. You don't do the job, you don't get the money."

"I did the job. I watched the store all night."

"You watch the wrong store, Tim. Insurance company don't pay if the cheaters get away cause you watch the wrong store."

"I got the license plate."

"Okay. You got the license plate. But the insurance company already knows who they are. License plate don't prove they got twenty thousand dollars of fire damaged computers. Just proves they got a license plate. I do got something for you though." Tito took a small stack of curled envelopes from the door pocket. "More mail come for you at the office. When you going to get an address people can know about Tim?"

"When you get me some work that pays?"

"Yeah, you know, that's going to be a problem. Insurance guys say I don't use you no more. Not after tonight."

"When did they tell you that, Tito, we've been together since you picked me up."

"Well, I'm pretty sure they going to tell me I don't use you no more."

"Oh. It's like that."

"You should at least get a better place, Tim." Tito took in the neighborhood, all small, detached houses looking very much like Tim's dump — unfinished. Most had garbage bags for windows and dirt lawns and either plastic siding or, at the point on the street when the banks gave up on the little Hispanic community, tar paper. "What you pay for that place, anyway?"

"Twenty-five a week. It's shelter."

"For a whole house you pay a hundred bucks a month? So that's why you live out here."

"Not the house. I live on the veranda, there." Tim pointed out an enclosed patio, partially clad with found materials from particle board to plastic sheets. "The rest of the house belongs to a fat Mexican couple and their five fat kids. I can't use the bathroom after eleven."

Tito looked at Tim. "Okay, Tim, serious, you need to go back to driving."

"I would Tito, I'd love to. God knows it's the only thing I was ever good at."

"So..."

"Well, there's gas, insurance, the three strikes law. I'm better off staying clean."

"Yeah, you really livin' it up Tim. Maybe you should sell the car then, if you not gonna drive no more."

Tim's almost new, low-profile, gray Malibu shone on the crumbling driveway, looking like a modern installation piece indicting the inequalities inherent in a capitalist society.

"It's all I've got. Anyway it's not mine to sell, really, not until I pay it off." Tim stepped onto the road. "Bye Tito. Thanks for the lift, at least."

"Maybe your luck gonna get better, Tim."

"You know Tito, I'd be happy to just negotiate a truce."

Tim gave his Malibu an apologetic tap on the fender as he passed and stepped into his enclosed veranda, looking forward to a morning nap and being out of the sun and little else. But he wasn't going to have even that much.

"Mike?" Tim's fat landlord, Miguel, was sitting on the couch/bed/only piece of furniture that wasn't a bar fridge, looking at Tim like he expected to be stabbed. Only slightly more strangely, Miguel also appeared at the interior door.

"That no Mike, Tim. That my little brother, Carlito. Carlito, this is Tim." Carlito smiled at Tim the way people who don't have guns smile at people who have guns.

"Okay. Hi Carlito. Mike, why is Carlito on my bed?"

"Oh, Carlito come to stay a while. Carlito, Carlito's wife. Their kids."

"I see. Going to be a little crowded here, isn't it Mike?"

"Little crowded. Yeah. Going to be a little crowded here." Mike took a serious interest in everything in the room but Tim.

"I'll just get my things, shall I?"

"You take your time, Tim. You take all day, if you want."

Tim was born in San Francisco and he spent his life and did his time there. So that's where he went now, to North Beach, specifically, with a vague plan to just be nearer the action, and hope that something turned up that didn't involve selling his car or stealing another one. He called his friends, and told them his tale and his situation and none of them were any help. He knew they wouldn't be. Some of them were real friends, but useless, and others were like Tito, and more useless, but they all had this in common — they were all bad for Tim and Tim's future and all they'd ever done for him is get him in trouble or get him jobs that didn't pay.

He sat in his car and watched the boats and girls and waves and the happy, sun-smeared features of the Bay, and he hated every stinking bit of it. He hated that he couldn't afford to live in the town he grew up in, or anywhere else for that matter. He hated his friends and the swelter and his life in California and he knew that he should just turn around and go, go east until his feet were wet. He promised himself that when he next got a stake together that's exactly what he'd do. But he knew that he was never going to get that stake together. Thus resigned, Tim fell asleep in his car.

So the tapping on the window entered his consciousness via a spontaneous dream that a cop was about to ask him to move on or show some ID or prove that he wasn't a vagrant or some equally catastrophic demand. But it wasn't a cop. It was kind of the opposite of a cop, in fact. It was Reggie the Bastard, one of the aforementioned friends, and he was about to change Tim's life.

Chapter 2

"Reggie." said Tim, as Reggie the Bastard let himself into the passenger side. "The Bastard."

"Tim." said Reggie The Bastard. "Tim the Nice Guy. How's that working out for you Tim?"

"I'm doing fine Reggie."

"Yeah, I know. I heard you were living in Malibu now. Oh, sorry, no, you're living in 'a' Malibu. I knew it was something like that. You want to turn on the air conditioning?" Reggie was attuned to the weather that way, because he always wore a baggy linen suit that neatly complemented his ample sweat glands over a patterned shirt and a light, leatherette holster, all over a gut that made him look like he could go into labor at any minute.

"I'm resting the engine. I hate to ask this Reggie, but do you have something for me?"

"I got five bucks for gas if you turn on the air conditioning."

Tim started the car. "That'll be five bucks."

"A bargain. How'd you like another 400 of those?"

"No."

"Just like that? No? You want to know what the deal is first?"

"I don't, Reggie, no. I already know enough. Anything that pays two grand is going to mean I break my number one rule about fighting battles I can't win. You've never offered me more than two hundred for anything that didn't involve a police chase."

"No? It must have been some other guy I paid a thousand to drive a truck across town."

"I did a year for that Reggie."

"You did?"

"Reggie, do you even know my name?"

"So maybe it's time I made it up to you. Two grand to take a quiet, no-nonsense drive to Mexico. A grand up front. All expenses paid. You can stay at the swankiest motels, eat at the finest truck stops."

"Reggie, I got two strikes. Two thousand isn't worth a fifteen year stretch."

"I didn't know that Tim. I'll throw in another five hundred."

Tim turned off the engine. "I'm afraid our time is up."

Tim took his mail and his five dollars to a taco stand and had the most satisfying burrito he could remember. He sorted through his depressing mail and discovered that if nothing else the events of the past 24 hours had enured him to the dispiriting effect of overdue alimony claims, orders to appear and repossession notices. He didn't bother opening them. The only mail that he didn't recognize by the return address of the law or lawyers was an elaborate cardboard press kit with a key-chain and full-color brochure for a high-performance 4x4 and an embossed invitation with his name written by hand. He liked it. Whatever it was, it was outside of the oppressive world of officialdom from which Tim hid like an itinerant strawberry picker, but in fact it showed promise beyond that.

The invitation was to legally do the one thing that Tim rarely did legally — drive fast. He was invited to participate in a promotional circuit of the Dakar, supposedly the fastest off-road vehicle in production. He just had to go to the track on Alameda — that evening — and take the car over one test circuit and then two real turns. If he gets the fastest time, he keeps the car. Second prize is the key-chain. There'd be press, probably, and even police, but there'd also be a buffet and a chance to climb out of debt in one, single turn around a dirt track. Tim put two dollars of gas in the Malibu before getting on the Oakland Bay Bridge, heading to Alameda, feeling like he'd maybe finally struck a deal with luck.

Tim parked outside a hangar at Alameda with a big vinyl banner over the door welcoming the press and participants to the preview test drive of the first stock 4x4 built intentionally for racing. There were hundreds of cars, worryingly, and even more worryingly were the police cars and press vehicles, but there was a soothing strength in anonymity and in any case things couldn't get much worse for Tim. He presented his invitation to the pretty plastic girls at the door and was directed to the buffet.

Taking in the competition, Tim felt optimistic. Few of them looked like serious drivers, mostly good old boys with baseball caps and a hungry look, some of them obviously drunk, others hiding it better. After about half an hour of resisting the donuts and the coffee that was weakening the reflexes of the other contestants, the lights went down and studio lights went up and a deep engine rev filled the room.

"Y'all like cars?" A big Texan, flanked by two bigger Texans, took to a podium at the front of the hangar and began playing the crowd. The crowd played back and roared their enthusiastic agreement that, yeah, they liked cars.

"But d'y'all like fast cars?" and again, the crowd was unanimous.

"Well then." said the big Texan, "Y'all got that in common. You know what else y'all got in common?" He waited for the silence that he seemed to be expecting, and Tim knew that something had gone terribly, terribly wrong. "Y'all are repossessed, and y'all are walkin' home." The Texans disappeared out a door behind them, the lights went up, and a palpable layer of dread settled on the crowd of deadbeat drivers.

The parking lot was empty. Empty of cars, at least. Personal possessions, including Tim's threadbare carpet-bag, lay on the steaming tarmac where the delinquent vehicles had been.

"Reggie? It's me, Tim."

"Four hours. That's longer than I expected you to hold out Tim. Where are you right now?"

"Alameda."

"How quick can you get to Sausalito?"

"About eight hours. I got no more wheels. Can you come and pick me up?"

"No, Tim, I don't drive. I hire people to drive. People like you. How come you got no wheels?"

"Someone wanted it more than me. You want me to drive you're going to have to give me a car."

"You make a lot of demands for a man in your position Tim. All right, a car, but I'm withdrawing the extra five hundred."

"You're a bastard, Reggie."

"Really Tim? Am I? No one's ever told me that before." said Reggie the Bastard.

Chapter 3

Ike Sugar was just that bit too physically and psychically tired to notice that anything was off when he got to his little house in San Antonio. He'd spent another day lying to the police, something to which he was ill-suited and unused, and he craved tranquility so much that when he saw the wallpaper peeling off the back living room wall he let himself believe that it was the heat, or the slapdash job he'd made of it only a few nights earlier. As he smoothed out his wall, though, reality forced its way through the mist.

"Evening, Ike."

Neatly out of view from anywhere but the center of the living room, his back to the mock fireplace, a mass of muscle in a department store suit stood, carving shavings out of an Sugar family heirloom onto the floor with a carpet knife.

Ike sized up the intruder. They were evenly matched. Both big, blond, crew-cutted heavy-weights, both sharp of jaw and clear of eye. But Ike had an extra ten years and fifty pounds of lazy on him, and the other guy had a carpet knife.

"Who are you?"

"I'm Eddie, Ike. Eddie Drucker. That name mean anything?"

Ike shook his head with a cautious sincerity. The name did not mean anything.

"What about Ray Costa? That mean anything to you?"

"You're not a cop."

"No, Ike, I'm not a cop." said Eddie. "But I was. I've been a cop, and I've been a con. And do you know how a cop named Eddie survives nine years in general pop for killing a gang-banger and copping his stash?"

As obscure a question as that may seem to anyone outside the correctional industry, Ike knew exactly how such a man survives. Ike, in his years as a guard at a state penitentiary, had seen it before and there's only one way that a man with a target on his head survives in the general population — by being harder and meaner than the hardest, meanest, most psychotic lifer in lockup.

"I already told the cops, I had nothing to do with Costa getting out. I don't know what happened."

"Yeah, you do Ike. And you're going to tell me what happened. I'm an insurance investigator Ike. Not official. Not really. So I don't care what you tell the cops, and I don't care about the, what is it? About ten grand you have hidden behind the wallpaper? But you're going to tell me how to find Ray Costa."

Ike squared off. He was an unmatched expert at sizing up situations exactly like this and there was a reason he was always on hand when the most dangerous prisoners were being moved or disciplined. He played it professional.

"What's that?" he asked.

"Unicorn." Eddie held up his work. "I think it used to be your state boxing trophy, 1982. I like working with oak."

"You put down the knife, we can talk."

Eddie put the knife on the mantlepiece among the remaining boxing trophies and photographs of semi-professional Ike Sugar in his prime.

"Fair enough. Now let's talk. The cops have to assume you're innocent. Talk to you nicely. I don't. So if you're going to take your shot, Ike, take it, and let's get on with it."

Reflexes get rusty and power gets pudgy but technique always remains with someone who dedicated as much time to a career in the ring as Ike Sugar. He crossed the room in an instant and caught Eddie square on the jaw with a point-perfect right hook. Ike knew a good connect when he felt it, and he felt one now, along with despair, because it was like hitting a concrete block — a concrete block who'd survived hard time.

Eddie bounced off the mantlepiece like the ropes of a ring, and was back in place, his expression unchanged and blank.

"I've been hit harder. A lot harder. And I can take it. And that, and a natural talent for and making and hiding sharp things, is how I survived nine years as the most hated guy in the general population."

"I got no idea where Costa is."

"I can believe that. But you know someone who does. Tell me that much and I'll leave."

"I got to live in this town."

"How do you think I found out about you Ike? The cops know you helped Costa escape, along with that girl from the prison clinic. She's gone. You're left holding the bag and a lousy ten grand that I found in five minutes. You're done here."

Eddie reached for the knife and Ike exchanged his boxing reflexes for his prison experience and folded his left for a throat punch that he'd used to subdue raging street-fighters. Eddie snatched it out of the air and spun its momentum into the wall and pinned it there with the horn of his unicorn.

Eddie put the carpet knife to Ike's throat. "You had your shot, Ike. Now tell me where to find Ray Costa."

Chapter 4

By 8pm the sun was as hot as it been all day on the shadeless Sausalito docks. Tim found his parking lot and called Reggie.

"I'm here, Reggie. Where are you?"

"Me? I'm in my pool Tim. You think this is concierge service? The car's there waiting for you. The keys are under the seat and there's an envelope in the trunk with your first thousand and an address."

"Fine. Which one is it?"

"Caddy."

"I see a dozen Caddies. Which one?"

"Coupe de Ville. Convertible."

"You're kidding."

"I know, sweet ride, isn't it? Take care of it. It's borrowed."

"Reggie it's pink. It's neon pink."

"So you can't miss it."

"You don't think a pink, convertible Coupe de Ville is a little conspicuous? The color alone is a misdemeanor east of I395."

"Yeah, you know, I'd have preferred something more low-profile. Say, a gray Malibu. You got a gray Malibu Tim?"

"What's at the address Reg?"

"Passengers. But it's too late to go now. Pick them up in the morning, head to Reno with the holiday traffic."

"Reno? I only have to go to Reno?"

"I said head to Reno, not go to Reno. You're crossing the border in Nevada."

"Why Nevada? I can be in Mexicali in a day."

"Tell you what, Tim, let's say the first thousand is for driving to Mexico, via Nevada, and the second thousand is for not asking me why you're driving to Mexico, via Nevada. Fair enough?"

The keys were under the seat and there was an envelope in the trunk with an address in the city and, as promised, a thousand dollars in fifties and twenties. Reggie the Bastard was a bastard, but he was bastard of his word. Tim decided to avoid the city until he couldn't anymore, and drove north up the shore for about twenty miles until he found a motel he could afford and where he could do laundry and clean up into something as closely resembling an innocent holiday traveler as he could manage. He couldn't change the car, but he could change his look to match it. He bought hair gel, a Hawaiian shirt and wrap-around sunglasses. He shaved and showered and ate tacos and drank cold, cold beer. And finally in the cool, dark, anonymous motel room, he felt good. In the mirror he felt like an idiot.

The address was a peeling and under-appreciated Queen Anne in the Mission District. The street was calm and reasonably empty of people and cars. Tim arrived at 10 under the spiteful sun with, against all his instincts, the top down. He stopped in front of the house and tried to look as laid back and natural as he could in a pink Cadillac with white seats carrying a two-time loser with slicked-back hair and a shirt printed with red and yellow hibiscus. He put a foot up on the dashboard. He played the radio. He tanned. Then he panicked when he heard the words that he's heard far too often and most lately in his worst nightmares.

"This your car, sir?"

A plain-clothed, featureless man in a brown suit had sidled up to the driver's side. He looked as much like an accountant as he did a cop. Maybe more so. On the sidewalk, standing the mandated twenty feet back, was his partner, a slim and square-jawed blonde in leather and jeans and with her hand ready by her hip.

Tim snapped up straight. "No."

"No?" said the brown haired voice of calm.

"No. It's a friend's. It's borrowed. I borrowed it to take some friends, some other friends, to Reno. For the weekend."

"I see. Can I see your license and registration sir?"

"Is there a problem?"

"No, no problem. It's just that you've been on this street for a while now, parked right here. In kind of a flashy car. Some neighbors think that amounts to suspicious behavior. It is kind of suspicious, don't you think?"

"No. Well, yeah, maybe, but I'm just waiting on friends. I got here early. They'll be along any minute."

"License and registration please."

So far as he knew the registration was good, but his license was not. If it were checked he'd be taken in for everything from unpaid alimony to missed court appearances. He looked in the glove compartment. It contained one bottle of vodka. Tim's luck was never kind, but it was consistent.

"Ah. That's right. The papers aren't in the car. They're at my friend's office. He's selling the car, and he was doing a lien search. I actually knew that, I just forgot. I can call him if you like."

"Not bad. How about the driver's license?" Not bad?

"That I have. Right here." Tim reached for his wallet when the blonde, seemingly on wheels, swooped to the passenger side and drew a nickel-plated .44 automatic that looked like a sewer pipe in her little hands.

"Hands where I can see 'em buddy."

Tim put his hands in the air. "It's just my license. I'm waiting for some friends. I'm not doing anything, I swear."

The man looked at his partner. "Okay?"

"He'll do. A little quick to panic, but he knows how to stick to a story."

"You're the pickup." Tim said, putting his hands down.

"Ray." said Ray, climbing into the back seat. "And this is Angel. Nice ride Tim. You got style. You dress like a Utah Shriner, but you got taste in cars."

An hour later they were across the bridge and an hour after that they were passed Sacramento and an hour or so after that Tim was starting to calm down.

"You don't talk a lot, do you Tim?"

Tim didn't bother to respond.

"I'm Ray Costa, Tim. You heard of me?"

"No."

"Okay, say you haven't. You know why I need to get to Mexico?"

"Honestly, Ray, I don't want to know. No offense, I'd really like to get this done as quickly and with as little hassle as possible. Emphasis on the limited hassle. I'd prefer not to get into the details but I'm at a point in my life where that's really important to me."

"No problem, Tim, that's what everybody wants. You know the way?"

"Mexico via Nevada. That's all I know. We're crossing into Nevada soon. Are we going by Reno?"

"Could do, if you want. The idea is to take it slow and easy and not take what anyone might describe as the obvious route. What do you think Angel? Reno?"

Angel, who had by now reclined the passenger seat and removed almost all her clothes and was tanning with quarters on her eyelids, said "Can we get married there? Like in Vegas? No questions asked?"

"I think they ask some questions, even in Vegas. That right Tim? Can you get married in Vegas, no questions asked?"

"You have to give your name and, in my experience, you have to be pretty drunk. Yeah, they ask questions. I don't think we should be stopping to get you married." said Tim, his eyes on the road.

"A honeymoon then. Just you, me, Tim and Baby."

"Baby?" said Tim. "Well, congratulations." It occurred to Tim to suggest they name the child Tim, because growing up on the lam in Mexico was just the sort of background you'd need if you wanted to turn out a man like him.

"Baby's my gun." said Angel.

"Suit up Angel." said Ray, turning back into the featureless man in the Mission District. "It's the law".

Sheriff Larry LaLande was a keen-eyed professional. A state-trooper for twenty-five years, he retired early to run for sheriff of the town where he lived just over the Nevada border. When the civil forfeiture trend caught on among law enforcement in the south Larry was just a small, powerless cog in a huge money-making machine, and he saw cash and vehicle seizures go to pay for police retreats and armored vehicles and state-of-the-art canteen facilities. He quit in disgust at fifty, ten years before qualifying for a full pension.

The practice of civil forfeitures is a legal gray area, tightly skirting the constitutional right to a fair trial by charging property, rather than people, with a crime. Cars and boats and cash have no standing before the law, and unless the rightful owners can somehow prove that their assets weren't being used in the commission of a crime — something that's about as hard to do as it sounds — they lose them for good, and they're sold at auction and the profits are divided up among the interested agencies.

So a Nevada trooper operating in the interests of the entire state would see little of the takings, and Larry wanted his piece of the pie. Now he had his own little stretch of highway between California and the nearest gambling mecca, rich with mugs carrying cash and probably doing other stupid things. And he was his own boss, made his own hours. He could go to work in a cowboy hat, and he did. He could get fat, and he did. And now he was surveying the I80 and employing an almost Holmesian capacity for spotting stupid people doing stupid things.

The neon pink drew his eye first and the hipster in the Hawaiian shirt third — second was what appeared to be a naked girl in the passenger seat. He lit up the roof and pulled onto the highway behind the Cadillac.

Angel was mostly dressed by the time Tim found a safe portion of the shoulder on which to pull off the road, the way a responsible driver does when hailed by the police.

"Just stick to the story you stuttered back in the city, Tim." said Ray, "Otherwise follow my lead."

"You folks know why I pulled you over?" said Larry, resting his stomach against the driver's side door.

"I hope so." said Ray. "You caught the guys who robbed us?"

"What's that?"

"We were robbed, sheriff. About two miles back. We pulled over to, well, you know, it's a long drive. We pulled over and we were out of the car maybe a minute when this pickup truck full of Mexicans stopped and took all our stuff right out of the car. Right there on the highway, with cars passing and everything. I've never seen anything like it."

"A truck full of Mexicans."

"Well, I assume they were Mexicans." said Ray. "I've never seen four guys riding in the back of pickup truck who weren't Mexican. They must have driven right past you. White truck. Dirty. With a big crucifix in the back window."

"Nope. Nothing like that went by." In fact Larry had seen at least three vehicles that day that could be described exactly as the truck Ray had just invented.

"We were on our way to the next town to report it. They got everything sheriff — all our cash, wallets, credit cards — everything was in our bags."

"They got all your money. Well, then, I think you folks best do your reporting in Reno. Next town along isn't really equipped to handle this sort of thing." said Larry, referring to his own fiefdom.

"But you're right here." Ray worked a credible squeak of grievance into his voice.

"And I'm afraid that this is where I have to stay. Highway robbery is a state thing. You'll get the help you need in Reno. Good luck to you folks."

And Larry went back to his car and his hunting.

Chapter 5

"That's the good stuff, Michael."

Steve Socorro over-poured two zombie glasses of whiskey and far too much ice for the good stuff. He was showing off, which is all he could really do these days. The boss has to stay aloof, above the extortion and retribution and bloodletting and all the other fun parts of gang life in Los Angeles. That's how you hold onto it, the good life, here in your Long Beach mansion. You surround yourself with guards and girls and you meet business associates like Michael on the deck of your pool, at a marble table, under a parasol. You don't ride your chopper anymore, you don't wear your colors anymore, you don't hit people over the heat with lead pipes, as much as you might miss it.

And you look like a boss, too. Steve was a massive, dark-skinned, scarred, tattooed and pony-tailed mountain of a boss but he wore tailored suits and silk shirts with a diamond pin instead of a top button.

But the suit was hot and the diamond pin scratched and the good stuff tasted like gasoline to Steve, no matter how much ice he put in it, and he missed doing what it took to get him where he is today.

Michael, being an under-boss, was free to stay street and he normally dressed like a gang-banger, but today he was meeting with the boss, so he was dressed like a pimp making a court appearance. He was hot and uncomfortable in his silk suit and snake-skin boots. And he was fiddling too much with his crucifix for a man relaxing poolside for a friendly business meeting.

"You like it? I got Champagne instead. I got everything. Yeah, you okay? Okay, good. Let's talk a little Michael."

Michael leaned forward and furrowed his brow. "Sure, Steve. What you wanna talk about?"

"The old days. You remember how we come up? On the east side? I told you this before, I know, but I always know I gonna be the boss."

"You always said that. And you were right."

"I was right. And there was only five of us then, but we didn't give no ground, and we moved up, and I always told you guys that you always move up with me. And I was right about that, too."

"Well..."

"No, I know, they all gone now, there's only you, but if they was here, you know, they'd be here. You know what I mean."

"Sure Steve. It's just bad luck."

"Not Handro."

"No, not Handro. He had it coming Steve."

"You remember Pipo?"

"Pipo? The Chilean guy who beat up the priest?"

"No, that's Pepito. Good guy, Pepito."

"Yeah."

"Yeah. No, Pipo. This is Pipo." Steve reached a giant hand behind his chair and came back with a lead pipe that had been recovered from a construction site, so it still had a lump of concrete forever fused to one end. Steve set Pipo softly on the marble table, like he was turning a page of antique bible.

"Oh. Right." said Michael. "Pipo."

"I find Pipo when I'm 14 years old, Michael. I know him longer than I know you. We got a lot of things done together, Pipo and me."

Michael put his drink on the table, freeing both hands to more efficiently manipulate his crucifix.

"Why you starting your own gang, Michael?" said Steve, his fingers resting lovingly on Pipo.

"I ain't Seb. I'm just recruiting some guys. Airport guys. For the gang. You know, I'm glad you asked me about it, cause I wasn't sure if I should be telling you the little stuff. You're the boss, Seb."

"These airport guys, they doing any jobs?"

"Yeah, I think. Maybe a couple."

"Like what?"

"Just little stuff, you know, baggage, some clip jobs. Some girls at the hotels. Little stuff."

"Little stuff. Like taking over the taxi concession?"

"Oh. That. Yeah, they might have done that too."

*And you think I don't find out, cause I'm down here on the beach and not on the street no more."

"Now, that's where you're wrong. I knew you were going to find out. Of course I knew."

"You know, maybe you did. Maybe you think by the time I find out, Michael's got his own gang, now Michael's the boss."

Michael wasn't without street skills of his own. He judged the situation, accurately, as a lost cause. He slumped in his chair and reached for his drink. He took a shaky sip. Then another. Then he hurled the glass at Steve and drew his gun from his pimp jacket. It was like sleight of hand, and it was beautiful, and it was too late. Steve was out of his chair and Pipo's stony, concrete head was connecting with

Michael's bony, fleshy head and coming out the clear winner of the conflict. Michael's eyes didn't have time to close.

Steve sat down with Pipo in his lap, and had another drink. His phone rang.

"Hey, good to hear from you. How are things in San Francisco?.. That's good to know... Fine, fine, nothing new. Oh, except I pick up the taxi concession at the airport...Oh yeah? When? How'd he get out?...Who's that? The Bastard? I never heard of him...No, I'll do it. Thanks though. Look you need to come down here sometime, I keep a bottle of the good stuff for you."

Steve ended the call and made another.

"Garry?" he said. "Get Garry. Come on over here. I need you to go to San Francisco."

Chapter 6

With only one working hand it took Ike Sugar all night to peel his life's savings out of the wallpaper. Not counting his trophies, everything he had after a boxing career cut short by throwing too many fights followed by almost thirty years as a prison guard was a little over $17,000 in small, sticky bills, mashed into a wad on his living room floor. And most of that he'd made in the last week. He pushed the bills into a gym bag and the trophies into a cardboard box and as such he was able to load his rusting Regal in one, single trip.

By noon he was on the road. He wasn't expected at work until Monday so unless the cops had more questions for him no one would notice that we was gone until then, when he'd already be in Reno and already set up working security for just enough under the table to keep food on it. It was better than jail and, in fact, just about anything is better than jail for a prison guard.

Nevertheless Ike was probably going a little too fast, even after he'd made it to the dubious sanctuary across the Nevada line. He knew better, but there was a certain minimum speed under which the dark forces at his heels took on a physical presence that felt like they were in the back seat, holding an oak unicorn.

Larry didn't usually concern himself with speeding. For one thing, this was an interstate, and not really his jurisdiction, but mainly speeding wasn't the sort of stupid that people carrying cash normally committed. But this rusting Regal was different in a way that triggered Larry's radar for the payoff. It was going just enough over the speed limit to betray a cautious desperation, there was that, but it was the driver as he passed that flipped the switch — his focused driving, his despondent look, his crudely bandaged left hand. Anyway it was a quiet morning.

"You know why I pulled you over?" Larry refrained from his usual intimidation tactic of resting his stomach on the driver's side door when he saw the mass of pudgy boxer behind the wheel. He kept a careful distance, from which he could see the man's hands but still look over the interior of the car.

"I guess I was speeding a bit. Sorry about that Sheriff. I guess I wasn't paying attention."

"Not paying attention is what gets people killed, son. What happened to your hand?"

"I uhm." It hadn't occurred to Ike to develop a back-story for his trip or his hand. "I cut it. On... something."

"Looks like someone cut it for you. You got anything in this car you're gonna wish you told me about before I find it?"

"No sir. Nothing."

"What's that, trophies?"

"Boxing trophies."

"You a fighter?"

"I was. Now I'm a guard. We're kind of in the same business. I'm a corrections officer. San Quentin."

"Uh huh. What about that bag?"

"Clothes. Just weekend clothes."

"Your clothes appear to be leaking. You want to step out of the car?"

Ike got slowly out of the car. He brought his experience to bear on the situation and judged it unwinnable. He knew what would happen if the sheriff saw his money, and he knew that the sheriff was going to see his money.

"Look, Sheriff, I'll tell you the truth. In that bag is all the money I've got. I'm blowing California, heading East.

"That so?"

"Yeah. Look, we're in the same business — you ever just get sick and tired of the low-lifes and scum and getting spit on for just doing your job? You ever just want to pack it all in and start over somewhere clean, where no one knows you?"

"Nope."

"Well, then, you're lucky. I'm not. So give me a break. Let me just go and I promise I'll watch the speed limit from here to Philadelphia."

"Let's see what's in that bag, first, then we'll see about who's giving anybody any breaks."

Ike pulled the gym bag from the back seat and opened it on the hood of the car.

"Why's it all sticky?" said Larry.

"It's wallpaper paste. I hid it in the wall, behind the wallpaper."

"That's pretty smart."

"I thought so too, once."

"How much is there?"

"Little over eight thousand." This was a fair ruse. In a wad of bills glued into a gym bag $8,000 looks about the same as $17,000. Sadly for Ike both amounts had exactly the same effect on Larry.

"Well you see my problem then. There's nothing illegal about driving down a highway with a cut hand and eight thousand dollars in sticky money, but there's something real suspicious about it. I can't charge you with a crime, but I can't just assume that this money isn't going to be used in the commission of one. That's the law."

It was not, in fact, the law, and Ike knew it. But Ike also knew that he was in no position to debate the point. What was he going to do, call a lawyer? He had nothing with which to bargain. Almost nothing.

"Look, Sheriff, I'm not a crook, but what if I had information about one? A big one."

"Do you?"

"I do. You know Ray Costa? The armored car robber?"

"No."

"It was a San Francisco thing. Five years ago. Four guys rob an armored car in the middle of the day and in the middle of the city. Killed a driver. Got away with millions. Only one guy gets caught — Ray Costa — and he's not talking. The money's still gone and he won't say where it is. Says he doesn't know, says he was betrayed by the other members of his gang, but the word is that it's the other way round. His gang's buried in the desert with the money."

"So?"

"So last week Ray breaks out of San Quentin. Way out. No sign of how he did it or where he's gone."

"And you know where he's gone."

"No. I don't know that. But I do know that he didn't leave San Francisco until yesterday, or maybe today. He was hiding out until the heat was off and he could drive out with the holiday traffic. And I know where he's going and how he's going to get there. He's going to Mexico. He's got a girl with him and a guy who's driving him in a big pink Cadillac."

Larry stopped at his concrete-block sheriff's office about ten miles off the 180 for only as long as it took. He was loath to waste a single second in pursuit of the pink Cadillac and the last seizure he'd ever need to make, but he felt that reinforcements were going to be a necessary precaution.

"Saddle up Nimrod. We got big game to hunt."

Nimrod was Rod, Rodney Dopple, Larry's deputy and son-in-law. Lacking any law-enforcement experience in general and in particular Larry's heightened capacity for spotting marks on the highway, his job was usually to keep up appearances at headquarters, answering the phone if it ever rang, and taking home a police income and a share of the take to keep Larry's only daughter, Vera, in overfed comfort. Nimrod was as skinny as a coke-addict, because he was a coke-addict, and he had a tendency to shake and no police uniform could give him an air of authority, but he could be trusted to do as he was told and to legitimately forget everything that he and Larry might do.

"Hi Larry." said Nimrod. "We going hunting? Cause Vera said no more hunting after I shot that cow."

"Nimrod, are you drunk?"

"Nope. Pretty high though."

"Rod, it's three o'clock."

"Already? Geez."

"In the afternoon."

"Oh. That's all right then. What's in the bag?"

"About eight grand."

"Why's it all sticky?"

"Wallpaper paste. Don't taste the money Nimrod."

"I was just checking."

"Get the shotgun, Nimrod, and lock up, and you know what? Bring the money. You can eat it on the way."

Chapter 7

"Me and my friends here were robbed on the highway."

It was a good story. It accounted for having no luggage and no ID and no credit cards, and it cast the teller in a sympathetic light.

"Sorry to hear that." said the clerk of the San-Doze Inn, a motel off the 180 in whose better days was still a low-rise, dusty and roach-infested last choice for those who were only slightly above sleeping in their cars.

"That's very nice of you sir. I really appreciate your kind words. And I hope you'll help us out."

"No credit. Sorry. It's forty bucks a night." The clerk didn't really look very sorry and he was, in fact, tremendously annoyed to be drawn away from the fan behind the desk of the cramped, aluminum clerk's office adjoined seemingly as an afterthought to the poured concrete shoebox of ten vacant rooms.

"Oh, no, of course not. I wouldn't even ask. Even if I needed to. I'm just a little too proud for that, I guess, even if I was just robbed right out there on the highway." Ray left out the Mexican part, unsure of the ancestry of the hairy, sweaty, under-shirted motel clerk. "I was just hoping that you'd let us pay cash. No credit cards, you see. No identification. We reported it to the police already."

"Forty bucks."

"We'll need two rooms."

"Eighty bucks."

"We really appreciate it." Ray handed over the money. "I'll just sign that register for you, if you like."

"Register?"

"Isn't that a register book?"

"Oh, yeah. I guess it is. If you want."

"I like to do things by the book. You never know when you'll be glad you did." Ray filled out the register and the clerk handed over the keys to the last two rooms, furthest from the road. Ray and Angel selected nine, leaving Tim with room ten. He parked the neon pink Cadillac in the dirt behind it, reasonably well hidden from the road.

"Air conditioning's broken." Tim turned the dials and tapped the uncovered filter on the antique brown box, held into a hole in the plain concrete wall by duct tape. "And the windows are nailed shut."

"Probably to prevent runners." said Ray. "Feels like home."

"I think it's paradise. I could live here forever." said Angel. "Just look at that." She stood at the window, looking out at the desert. "That's what forever looks like."

"I'm not sure why we had to stop at all." said Tim. "I'd be just as happy, happier even, to drive all night."

"It's like I said, Tim, we're taking it slow." said Ray. "I'd have preferred to stay in San Francisco a while longer, in fact, but my friends there were getting less and less reliable."

"Yeah, I know what that's like."

"I need ice. " said Angel.

"There isn't any. I checked." said Tim. "We're going to have to satisfy ourselves with warm beer."

"For the beer? I need it for a bath."

"You want to take an ice bath?"

"Give me the keys. There was a gas station. They'll have ice."

"No." said Tim. "No keys, no ice, no leaving the motel. Okay?"

Angel looked at him like he'd just told her she was too fat to be a ballerina, and held that look for a disturbingly long time before curling up on the bed with her gun to her breast. "Not much longer now, Baby." she said, so quietly that the gun could barely hear it.

Tim looked at Ray with a face that said this person is crackers and Ray looked back with one that said, yeah, he knew that already.

"I'm going to our room, then." said Angel, suddenly channeling a sane person, and she left.

"What?" said Tim.

"She's okay." said Ray. "You just can't overfeed the fire."

"I'll keep it in mind."

"Anyway she's been good for me, and unlike my friends in San Francisco, I can trust her."

"If you say so."

"I can. She's in love with me. Says we're soul mates. She helped me get out the joint."

"So it's a prison break. I was afraid of something like that. I told you I didn't want to know."

"Oops. Too late. Now you know. Want to know more?"

"Oh, what the hell." Tim opened another beer.

"I've been in for five years. Armored car job. My role was simple — I was the patsy. I'd never done anything before, but I was down on my luck, recently divorced, laid-off. I was in real estate, got in just as the market crashed and burned. I'm lucky that way."

"Been there." said Tim.

"Yeah, I figured. Anyway I get left holding the bag, and the bag is empty."

"You spill?"

"I would have. I tried to. The prosecution offered me a pretty good deal, too. They knew I wasn't the brains behind the job. But, and this is the genius part, everything, absolutely everything I knew about the other guys, was made up. They took me to their homes, introduced me to their wives, we went bowling. Then when I told the cops everything I knew, everything I knew turned out to be a lie."

"That is pretty clever."

"In an evil, cold-blooded kind of way, yeah, it is. I still sort of hold a grudge, though. I'm petty that way."

"What about the nut bar?"

"Angel? She worked in the prison. She was my therapist."

"What kind of therapy?"

"Psych. Rehabilitation. Kind of pointless for a twenty year stretch, but prison, I suspect you know, has its peculiarities."

"She's a psychiatrist? Angel?"

"Angela, actually, and a psychologist, with a speciality in criminal minds. Yeah."

"Wow."

"I know. But she compartmentalizes. Total professional around the guards, but one-on-one she's going on about past lives and how she and

I were once Eloise and Abelard or two Beluga whales or whatever came to her in a dream the night before."

"And she got you out. All by herself."

"God no. We had a lot of help. It took a lot of grease."

"I don't care, and don't tell me if it's going to complicate my life, but if you don't have the job money, where'd you get the grease?"

"I didn't. Or rather, it's borrowed, in a manner of speaking. I figured if no one's going to believe I don't have a big pile of cash buried in the desert, why not leverage that? I mean, everyone thinks I'm this criminal mastermind anyway..."

"But what happens when your creditors come looking for a return on their investment?"

"I'll let you know."

"Please don't."

Both men were startled to a standing position at that very moment by the unmistakable sound of a gun being fired, a big gun, followed swiftly by another and then another, from somewhere behind the motel. They looked at each other and then fell immediately to the floor. Ray crawled to the window.

"You see anything?" whispered Tim.

"I do."

"What is it? Cops?"

"No, it's not cops."

"What then?"

"Have a look yourself." Ray stood, accompanied by more gunfire.

Tim crawled to the window. "What the hell is she doing out there?"

"Taking Baby for some exercise, would be my guess."

"She's completely naked."

"Communing with the desert."

"She's going to get us killed, Ray."

The gunfire settled, eventually, and Tim hoped it meant that Angel was completely out of ammunition. And all was cool, beer drinking silence.

The sound of a car pulling onto the gravel driveway of the motel broke the vigil, and Ray went to the front window. He peered through the curtains.

"Just a guy. Traveling salesman, looks like. Look, I'm going to go see about Angel. If she's done acting crazy she'll probably want to talk crazy for a while."

"Better you than me."

"Right about that." said Ray, and left the room.

The thing about hunches is you only have to dig a little deeper to find that they're usually the manifestation of experience, an acquired ability to pick up on subtle clues or probabilities that aren't anywhere near as mysterious as the word implies. Eddie's hunch about the San-Doze Inn, for instance, was pure logic. Anyone lying low on the road to Reno is going to avoid places with a lot of people and only the sleaziest motels are going to let you stay without showing at least some sort of identification, and probably producing a credit card.

"Hiya." said Eddie.

The clerk once again separated himself reluctantly from his fan.

"Afternoon."

"I'm hoping you can help me. I'm looking for someone. Anybody check in recently? In the last few hours, say?"

"You a cop?"

Eddie smiled at the clerk, his hands on the counter. "Does it matter?"

"Three people, couple hours ago."

"They sign the register?"

"No. Actually, yeah, they did. Made-up name though."

"Really? How can you tell?"

"You get to know these things."

"May I?" Eddie opened the register. No one had signed it for years, but neatly printed on a fresh page was a single line with the current date and the name "Rob Serious, Room 10".

"Thanks." said Eddie.

Tim opened the door, expecting to see Ray and, probably, Angel, knocking and wanting to talk. Instead it was a big, blond crew-cutted, official-looking block that Tim immediately assumed was the law.

"Hello Ray." said Eddie.

"You got the wrong room, I think." said Tim.

"No, Ray, I have the right room. You signed the register, which tells me two things — you're Ray Costa, and you're an idiot." He pushed the door open and Tim offered no vain resistance, as the pieces fell painfully into place.

"I'm not Ray. I'm Tim. Ray's in the next room."

"Tim, you say. I learned a third thing, Ray, you are really bad at making up names."

"It's Timothy."

"Well that's better. I'd heard that you were this brilliant liar, could make up a story on the spot more convincing than the truth. Sit down Ray."

Tim sat down in the only chair in the room. "I'm really, really not Ray. He's in the next room. With Angel."

"Okay, you're not Ray Costa. Where is he then?"

"I just said. He's in room nine."

"That would be the room right next to this one?"

"Yes."

"The one with the door open and not a soul inside it?"

"Yeah, that wouldn't surprise me." Tim looked at the window sill, where he'd left the car keys. There were no car keys.

Eddie kept a comfortable distance and he left the door open. He sat on the bed.

"You know who I am?"

"No. And please don't tell me."

"I'm Eddie Drucker. I'm an insurance investigator. I've been on a cold trail for the entire time that you've been in the can. Now you're out and the trail is hot again. And you're going to direct me the rest of the way."

"I would. I swear to God I would, but I'm not Ray Costa. I'm Tim Morro, I'm just the driver. I didn't even know who Ray Costa was before today."

"If I were a cop — and I know this because I used to be a cop — I'd have to take your word for that. Assume you're innocent. I'm not a cop anymore, Ray. And I don't have to be nice. Which is good, because nice isn't really in my nature." Eddie took his carpet knife from his pocket and slid out a length of new blade. Tim eyed the door. Eddie followed his glance.

"Like your chances Ray? Take your shot, and let's get this started."

"That's okay."

"Sure?"

"Sure."

Eddie shrugged, got up and closed the door. He approached Tim and took the little finger of his left hand in his huge fist, bending it back until tears were streaming down Tim's cheeks. He leaned over until his mouth was at Tim's ear.

"Where is it Ray?" he whispered.

"I swear to you, I don't even know what it is. I don't know where anything is."

Eddie placed the blade at the acutely angled joint between Tim's little finger and the rest of Tim. "I think you need to know that I'm serious." he said, and cut off Tim's finger.

Eddie sat down on the bed to let Tim scream and cry and eventually run to the bathroom to wrap his hand in a yellowing towel. Tim returned to the room and stood, shaking with pain and rage.

"You... you. You give that back." He said, unsure of what he was trying to express.

"I think it rolled under the bed. You're welcome to look for it, but it won't be the last one, unless you're ready to talk. And even then, honestly? No guarantees."

There was a knock at the door. Eddie looked at Tim and put a finger to his lips. Tim endeavored to stifle the weeping.

Eddie walked softly to the door and put his hand gently on the knob. In a single move he pulled the door open, reached out and grabbed the collar of what turned out to be a skinny coke-addict in a police uniform, who reflexively kneed Eddie in the groin. Eddie absorbed the shock like a mannequin, but was briefly frozen in time and space and, later, he would recall that he went temporarily blind.

The scuffle entered the room, with Sheriff Larry LaLande taking up the rear guard with a shotgun. In seconds, Eddie had recovered and had his carpet knife to Nimrod's throat and would have opened it had Larry not grabbed his wrist, turning the three of them into a single, mangled standoff.

Tim took it in as rapidly as he could, but his instincts were quicker than his mind. There was no getting past the many-headed monster in the doorway, the windows were nailed shut, he was unarmed. Tim kicked the delicately balanced air conditioner through the wall and dove out after it. Larry found just enough freedom of movement to fire a load of shot after him.

"Let's go Tim." Angel was behind the wheel of the Cadillac. Ray was in the passenger seat. Tim high-jumped into the back and the wheels kicked up a cloud of desert dust.

Larry dropped the shotgun and pulled his service revolver and put it to Eddie's eye, which went some distance to bringing calm to the situation.

"Sit down, you," said Larry. Eddie sat on the bed, preferring to avoid the blood soaked wooden chair.

"Nimrod, pick up that gun." Nimrod picked up the shotgun and steadied it, as well as he could, on Eddie. Nimrod seemed to be having the time of his life.

"You watch him." said Larry. "I don't know who this guy is but you can bet he knows something. Do not let him leave here, you understand me Rod?"

"He ain't going nowhere Larry, not in one piece."

"Don't kill him neither, Rod, you hear me? I'll be back."

Larry ran to the cruiser parked, from his perspective, far too far away, by the motel office. So Tim and Angel and Ray had a very convincing head start by the time he made it to the highway, and he could barely see them in the distance. He put the lights on and he floored it.

"Do you know who I am?" asked Eddie.

"Nope." said Nimrod.

"I'm Eddie Drucker. I'm an insurance investigator. This is just a misunderstanding. I think we're on the same side here."

"Well, we'll see about that when the sheriff gets back, okay? You just take it easy. Have a little nap if you want."

"Yeah, I don't think so. I think you might have crippled me. You got any meat on that knee at all?"

"Not much."

"Are you okay? I'm sorry if I hurt you. You look a little shaky."

"I'm doing just fine."

"You sure? You look like maybe you need some medicine of some sort. You got any medicine? Rod? Is it?"

"I might. You just keep your distance and maybe I got a little medicine for both of us."

"That'd be great. What you got?"

Nimrod switched the shotgun to his left hand and fished around in his pocket. He withdrew it with a little tobacco tin, the sort used for chewing tobacco, among those who chew tobacco. Nimrod didn't chew tobacco. He put the tin on top of the television and pinched out enough for two lines and used Eddie's carpet knife to form them.

"Got a bill?" he asked Eddie.

"I do." Eddie took a twenty out of his wallet and made a point of reaching across a safe distance to hand it to Nimrod.

"Wow, that smarts." he said, remaining hunched and massaging his groin. "I think you popped one."

"Ew. Really?" said Nimrod, expertly rolling the bill with his free hand.

"Yeah. Seriously. A little of that pain killer would do me some good." He reached his hand inside the front of his pants and massaged his injury.

"Sorry, man, really." said Nimrod, bending to take a snort. And while he did Eddie withdrew his hand and with it a small wooden shiv.

"He cut off my finger. You bastard. You were out there all the time while he cut off my finger."

"I'm truly sorry about that Tim." said Ray. "I had no idea that was going to happen."

"You knew something was going to happen. You led him right to me — did you or did you not sign your name on my room number?"

"I did." Ray ceased being distracted by the absence of police lights in the distance. They had left Larry in the dust and in fact the Sheriff was already on his way back to the motel to collect his deputy and pick up the trail in Reno.

"You need to understand why I did it, Tim. When you understand you won't be so mad."

"No, I'm still going to be this mad. I'm always going to be this mad."

"No, you're not Tim, because remember when I said that I didn't know where the money was? From the robbery? Well I do. I know where it is, all of it. And they know I know. If that guy had gotten hold of me he'd have gotten it out of me eventually. You see? You couldn't tell him where it is, because you don't know where it is."

"Wait. The money." said Tim.

"That's right. More than enough to buy you a new finger."

"No, my roll. It's back in the motel."

"Oh, that money. That a problem?"

"It is if you want to get to Mexico."

"Then it's a problem. In the meantime we need to do something about your hand. You know anyone in Reno Angel?"

"I know people everywhere Ray."

"Reno it is."

"Wait." said Tim, "Stop at the next phone. I've got to make a call."

"A thousand dollars? No, Tim, you get the rest when the job is done, that was the deal."

Tim was in pain and impatient but Reggie the Bastard wasn't picking up on the urgency of the situation.

"Okay, fine then. I'm done. You can pick your car up in Reno."

"Calm down Tim. I'll make it five hundred. How do you even wire money to a hotel? Do they do that?"

"Make it a thousand, Reggie. It's got a casino. Wire it to the casino. Don't use my name. Use yours."

"Okay. Five hundred. Name of Reggie the Bastard."

"A thousand Reggie. They'll give you a code number. Call me at the hotel when you've got it. I don't have my phone anymore, so ask for Connie at the front desk. Apparently she's friends with Angel."

"You lost all your money? You lost your phone? What else you lose Tim?"

"The little finger off my left hand."

"You still got the Caddie though, right?"

"Did you hear what I just said?"

"Tim, how off the rails is this thing?"

"There are no more rails, Reggie."

"That bad, is it?"

"Just send the money, Reggie, and do it quick. I don't want to spend any more time in one place than I have to."

Chapter 8

Garry Abernathy and Garry Avila were brothers in every way except that they weren't brothers. They dressed alike — black suits, white silk shirts, black ties — and over the years they'd grown to look alike, too, even though Garry was Hispanic and Garry was mulatto. They both shaved their heads — Garry, because he was balding, and Garry because Garry shaved his head, because he was balding. They both had black handlebar mustaches and even had a similar, vicious scar on their right cheeks. It was said that Garry scarred himself deliberately after failing to protect Garry in a bar fight which resulted in a vicious scar on his right cheek. This wasn't true, however, and neither Garry had ever lost a bar fight. And they were both in the same line of work — they were enforcers for Steve Socorro.

So the effect on Reggie the Bastard when he saw the Garrys step out of his house and onto the deck of his pool was such that he took an instinctive glance at his drink, as though suspicious what might be in it, or how many he'd had.

Reggie floated in his pool in a big inflatable donut, with a dozen little inflatable donuts all around him, for his phone, a laptop, drinks, a television set, cocaine — all the necessities of the home office. He paddled himself until he was facing the Garrys, who stood poolside.

"Whatever you're selling," said Reggie, "I'll take two."

"Where is Ray Costa?" said Garry.

"Who?" said Reggie, and instantly regretted it. The Garrys drew their guns and systematically sank almost the entirety of Reggie's flotilla.

They let the echo die down and the smoke clear.

"Where is Ray Costa?" said, possibly, the other Garry.

"Ray Costa. The guy who escaped from San Quentin last week. You think I know where he is?"

The Garrys torpedoed the remaining satellite vessels. There was only Reggie, floating amongst the wreckage.

"Okay. Stop already. I got nothing to do with that but — " he raised a 'don't shoot' hand as the Garrys raised their guns again "— but I think I know where he's at. Or where he's going to be soon enough."

The Garrys lowered their guns again.

"There's a hotel. In Reno. The Claim. He's got a girl with him, Angel, and a guy doing the driving named Tim. You guys want to get there before they leave your best bet is a plane."

"Mr. Socorro appreciates your cooperation."

"Socorro? Steve Socorro?"

The Garrys nodded again.

"What's he want with Ray Costa? I'm just asking."

"You really want to know? Cause we can tell you, if you really want to know." The Garrys raised their guns again.

Chapter 9

The Claim Hotel and Casino is on the western access to Reno and only technically within the city limits. It's a featureless, brick two-story lack of inspiration with a vast parking lot, a restaurant and a casino. In any other context it would house cut-rate law offices and maybe an optometrist. It's a drab, ugly, cynical run-off operation even by the standards of Reno, Nevada, which is the hotel-casino equivalent of looking pitiable next to an LA wino. It was the perfect place for Ray and Angel and Tim to lay low and wait for Reggie to send them gas money.

Even the neon pink Coupe de Ville was reasonably well camouflaged in a parking lot populated by other flamboyant convertibles and a fiberglass forest of recreational vehicles. And Tim could hide out in the cool, dark room with a view of the parking lot, made possible by Angel's acquaintance with the hotel staff. Ray and Angel, on the other hand, were gambling, presumably having somehow persuaded the house to extend them a line of credit.

Tim had bandages and painkillers and a sense of loss for his pinkie finger that could best be described as sentimental. It's not a finger, he felt, that he'd sufficiently appreciated while he had it. And now it was mouse-food, under bed in a cheap motel on the I80. Judging by the standards of hygiene at the San-Doze Inn, his finger's last act on this earth would probably be to scare the hell out of a traveling salesman looking for a sock. Not a fitting end, for a finger which gave so much and asked so little.

The beer and hydrocodone weren't so much killing the pain as diverting it into sentimental reflection about lost digits and a larger, melancholy musing on Tim's situation in general. On the unbroken string of bad decisions and worse luck that end with him bleeding in a Reno warehouse hotel, on the Malibus, bankrolls and the fingers he's left in his wake, on the fact that it'd been hours since he gave Reggie the Bastard a ten minute job to do.

"What the hell are you doing Reggie?" said Tim, before Reggie got the phone to his ear.

"What? I'm not doing anything at all? What would I be doing?"

"Wiring me a thousand dollars."

"What? I did. It's not there yet? Did you check?"

"Reggie you were going to call me with a code. Do you have the code?"

"Code? Oh, right. Yeah, I got that."

"Good. Tell it to me."

"Okay, ready? You writing this down? Six, Six, Seven, Eight, Six, Gee for Giraffe..."

"Reggie."

"What?"

"Start again."

"What? Why?"

"Just start again."

"Okay, uh, Six, Six, Six, Eight, Gee for Giraffe..."

"Reggie you bastard. What have you done?"

"What have I done? What have you done? You were supposed to take two people on a quiet drive through Nevada, raise no flags, drop no crumbs. And now I got cookie cutter killers draining my pool for me."

"Reggie, one of these guys, was he a big blond guy with short hair and a thing for knives?"

"Big, yes, everything else, no. Two bookends — bald guys with tight suits and matching 'staches and fencing scars. They shot at me in my pool, Tim. In my pool. I think I got PTSD."

"Reggie you got to send me my money. Do it right now."

"Yeah, I'll get right on that Tim."

"Reggie, you don't top me up then this thing is over. I know you financed this guy's bustout and if you want to see any of that pay off you're going to have to carry me to Mexico."

"Ha. Tim, It's already over. You know who sent those guys to fill my pool with lead? Steve Socorro. You know who that is?"

"No."

"Okay, good. I'm jealous of you. Live out your days in tranquil innocence. Me? I'm cursed with knowing what this guy can do with a half a length of lead pipe and the slightest provocation. When he finds out that I got this joker out of the joint, I don't know what he's going to do, but I hope it's over quick."

"Yeah, that's real rough for you Reggie. Listen, if these guys catch up to me, you want me to tell them that? That you hope it's over quick?"

There was a significant pause in the conversation.

"Tim you got to get out of there."

When Tim found Angel she was in the sun room lounge, telling the fortunes of a busload of Canadian senior citizens. She sat in a white wicker peacock chair looking like a moth princess, clasping the hands of a withered snow bird who wanted to know if, according to the spirits, today was a good day to spend feeding her children's inheritance into a bottomless slot machine or would it be better to throw it across the tricked out Blackjack table with the auto-shuffler.

So when Tim leaned over and cupped his hand over her ear and Angela cocked her head with a quizzical air, the effect on her audience was only to enhance her credentials.

"Very well." she said, "I understand. You may leave me."

She turned to her rapt Winnipeg seniors. "I must leave you now, but go, go and stick with the table games."

The casino floor of the Claim is immense and low and like most casinos it's lit from the ceiling with low-frequency, high-glare, yellow neon lights, designed to discourage looking up from the table. This makes searching for someone at a casino, as an exercise, strikingly similar to looking for your keys on a sunny beach with hangover.

And in fact it wasn't Ray that Tim saw first, it was the Garrys. They were standing at the well-tread nylon carpet trimmed with plastic palm trees and defining the border between the huge table gaming area and the electronic gaming area which dwarfed it. They were perpendicular to each other, forming a panoramic lookout and resembling one man in a tailor's mirror. Tim recognized them instantly from Reggie's hysterical description. He saw Ray next, maintaining a party atmosphere around a Blackjack table and, it would appear, winning.

"Go get the car. Bring it to the door." said Angel.

"Angel, let's just get Ray and go. Those guys haven't spotted him yet. We can slip out quietly."

Angel looked at him with a little smile on only one side of her mouth. A little smile that just about anywhere else and at any time and on anyone less crazy would have struck Tim as quirky and charming. But now, in this place and in this moment and on this girl, it made Tim's blood run cold. She held the gaze for a beat and a half, turned to the giant hall and said "Ray. Hey, Ray. Over here. Hi Ray." as loud as she could.

"I'll go get the car." said Tim.

"Hi Honey."

"Hi Angel."

"Winning?"

"A little, yeah. Why did you call my name from across the room?"

"To warn you. You see those two guys in black suits and mustaches?"

"Do they look like pit bosses but not as hateful?"

"That's them. They're here to kill you."

"You know Angel, that doesn't sound like a reason to yell my name across the room. In fact, that sounds more like a solid reason to not yell my name across the room."

"It's part of my plan. You stay here. I'm going to the ladies' room."

"Is that the plan or just something that you need to take care of?"

"It's the plan. Part of it. You see the the ladies', directly across from here?"

"Yeah."

"With palm trees on either side of the door?"

"Palm trees. Yes. I see it."

"You can. And from here you're just about the only one who can. Keep your eye on that door."

Angel left Ray at the table with his new Blackjack friends and he was soon joined by the Garrys, who stood on either side of him and watched him play, by all appearances genuinely intrigued by the complex mathematical ballet of trying to get near twenty-one without going over. Ray played blindly, looking intently in front of him, waiting for a sign. He felt the Garrys get closer and palpably more threatening until everything was just the Garrys, the glare, the din, and the door. Presently the door to the ladies' room swung slowly open and there was Angel, drawing her nickel-plated .44 from her purse and pointing it directly at Ray. Ray looked right down the barrel. He nudged the Garrys lightly. "Is that chick pointing a gun at us?"

As the Garrys drew their weapons Ray retreated and fell out of one character and into another. "This is a hold up." he said, with a booming authority that came from everywhere, and all eyes were on the Garrys.

And then the screaming started, followed in a single measure by the stampeding, the hoarding of chips, and the exchange of gunfire — some from the Garrys, but most from legal Conceal and Carry permit holders having a nice, constitutionally protected day out at the casino.

Even before the shooting stopped, Tim and Ray and Angel were on the 395, heading south.

Chapter 10

Of course, not all hunches are right, even when they're based on the sound logic that Ray would want to avoid Reno where Larry might have warned the local law. The flaw here was simply that Eddie failed to take into account that Larry was now less of a law enforcement officer, and more of a rival.

And yet it paid off, in that Eddie had left the 180 for a regional highway, with the intention of circumventing Reno and catching up to Ray on the 395 going south, and he made this maneuver not minutes before Larry would have otherwise passed him, on his way back to the San-Doze Inn. Still, it was just a hunch and, as such, incomplete. When Eddie got to the to the southern tip of Reno he had a judgment call to make. The 580 was a freeway, direct, unfettered. The Carson-Reno Highway was a cow-path, but it had the dubious advantage of being less-traveled, particularly by state troopers.

Past the ranches and ranch suppliers this stretch of the Carson-Reno Highway is little but scrub-land on either side until you see the Sierra Nevada in the west. There's little cover, few places to pull off, not even a lot of gas stations.

The sun was still high enough and hot enough to simmer little mirages off the surface of the road and the traffic was thin. Even that which there was of it was mostly local — some horse trailers and bale trailers and a few bikers getting their American Experience. Eddie was beginning to doubt what amounted to a coin-toss that made him choose the highway.

He stopped at a gas station and filled up. Then he stepped inside the little aluminum shed to pay and test a theory.

"Thanks." said Eddie, pocketing his change. The girl behind the counter showed promise. She was maybe sixteen, and she resented being made to work what was probably her daddy's gas station franchise on a Saturday evening when all her friends, presumably, were out cow-tipping or at the big barn dance. So she'd been resting her chin in her hands and watching the traffic go by since Eddie pulled in and she returned to doing that now.

"I missed some friends up in Reno. Meant to be going to Carson to meet up with other friends. I wonder if you've seen them."

The girl stayed perfectly stationary but for her eyes, which looked heavenward and communicated a simple message — she didn't know what his friends looked like, and she didn't care to.

"You won't have missed them if they went by. Three of them, in a big pink convertible."

She looked strangely surprised and did Eddie the honor of standing up straight.

"Well, yeah." she said. "Right there."

And indeed, in that moment Tim and Angel and Ray were pulling up alongside Eddie's car on the other side of the pumps. Eddie realized that he'd left Nimrod's shotgun in the car and a carpet knife was little use at that distance. But with the pumps between Eddie and the Cadillac there was just a chance.

"Thanks, Miss." he said and left the shed.

"Anybody got any money?" said Tim.

"I do." said Angel, taking her purse from under her seat.

"How much? Enough for a tank of gas?"

"Uhm." She shuffled about the contents of the purse, taking Baby out to make the job easier. "About four thousand dollars."

"What? Where did you get four thousand dollars?"

"Savings. Wise investments."

"No, I mean, why didn't you mention that you had a stake? Why did I have to call Reggie?"

"How should I know why you had to call Reggie? Maybe you missed him."

"Amazing. I'll pump, you pay." And in that instant Tim turned and saw Eddie, standing on the other side of the pumps, on the other side of his car, with a shotgun in his hands. They took each other in and Tim's heart raced and his hand throbbed in a reflex and rapid internal conflict between running and revenge. Running would doubtless have won out, but Angela was already on her knees in the passenger seat, Baby in hand, level next to Tim's head. She shot out the passenger side tires of Eddie's car. Tim only heard the first shot. By the second his eardrum had been burst and he momentarily forgot Eddie, his hand and his name.

"Go." said Ray and Angel as one. He sort of heard Ray. He didn't need to. In a moment the car was back on the road.

Chapter 11

Larry had a hunch, too. His hunch was that the dozen or so police cars in the parking lot of the Claim Hotel-Casino on the road into Reno might have something to do with Ray or Eddie and probably both. He wove his car through the crowd and up the cordon. The parking lot was packed and people were standing about sharing, embellishing and generally polluting their witness statements.

"What happened here?" Larry asked a patrolman at the casino entrance.

"Inside city limits, I think, Sheriff."

"I know. Just caught my eye. I was on my way to the station in Reno. Pursuing a suspect. Killed my deputy, officer."

The patrolman took off his sunglasses and became a fellow cop. "I'm sorry to hear that Sheriff. We had a shootout here. Right on the floor of the casino. It's a mess."

"Get the guy?"

"Maybe. Hard to tell. We're hearing everything from a lone bandito trying to rob the casino all by himself to a cartel hit. No two stories the same. One shooter's dead, that much is for sure."

"What'd he look like? The shooter." Larry wasn't sure if he wanted it to be Eddie or not.

"Dunno." said the patrolman. "You want to have a look? He's already bagged."

"Yeah, if you don't mind."

The patrolman led Larry to the coroner's van. "Mind if the Sheriff has a peak? He might have an idea who the guy is." They climbed inside the van and Larry unzipped the black body bag. It wasn't Eddie, nor anyone else even like anyone he'd seen before. The man was big, bald and well-dressed, with a biker's mustache and an ugly scar down his right cheek.

"Nope." said Larry. "Not my guy."

"Worth a shot. You want me to get someone to take your APB? I can't, not right now, but they'll take care of you at the station."

"That's all right. He's not going stick around Reno anyway, not with all this going on."

"That's probably true. Still, there's state."

"That's my next stop. Thanks for your help. Good luck with all this."

"Yeah. You too Sheriff."

Larry surveyed the crowd and the cars and nothing spoke to his memory or instincts. It wasn't until he looked to the road and the almost completely deserted parking lot across the street that he saw what absolutely had to be a sign. He got closer, to be sure, that the man he was seeing standing on the other side of the street, arms crossed and, possibly, weeping, was the man he'd just seen in a body bag. He watched in amazement as the man put his sunglasses back on and get in his car. There was no getting out of the parking lot in time for a pursuit, so Larry went close enough to the road to watch the black Ford saloon, probably a rental, get on the 395, heading south.

Chapter 12

Steve stood at the deck of his pool, drink in one hand, phone in the other, listening. Then, when he was done listening, he put his phone in his pocket, and poured his drink into the pool. He dropped the glass in after it.

It was too hot and too close to be standing, inert and ineffective, in a garden in a three-layered suit and a shirt that doesn't breathe and done all the way up to the neck. He left the pool and went to his house, to his room, into his closet, which was almost another room, with smaller closets built into three walls, mirrors, and an upholstered bench in the middle. He took off all his clothes and left them on the floor and slid open the closet on the left, by the door. He took out his jeans, his jacket, his boots and bandana — his colors — and he draped them over the bench.

Transformed, he descended to the garage, collecting Pipo on the way. He looked like the Steve who wanted a beach house now, not the Steve who lived in one. He moved with freedom and he sounded like chains when he walked. He passed the Lexus, the BMW, the Hummer. He pulled the tarpaulin off his motorcycle — a matte gray Harley Davidson V-Rod, lovingly oiled and polished and ignored for years.

And he was on the street, back in LA, proudly wearing his colors in the city he conquered wearing them. And soon after that, he wasn't anymore — he was on the Barstow Freeway, heading north.

And Garry was on the Carson-Reno Highway, heading south. The distance and the available freedom of movement between Garry going south from Reno and Steve heading north from Los Angeles was getting smaller at a combined 200 miles an hour. But at about the same point on the road and for the same reason Garry began to suspect he should be on the almost parallel 580. He pulled into a gas station to top up the tank and canvass the locals.

"Hi." Garry said to the pre-startled girl behind the counter in the little aluminum shed. "Tell me something — have you seen a pink convertible Cadillac Coupe de Ville pass here in the last couple of hours? Would have been carrying two or three people."

The girl nodded with a manner and a look that caused Garry to conclude that she was simple.

"You did? You sure? A pink Cadillac."

The girl nodded, more aggressively now.

"Going south."

Further nodding.

"Get gas?"

The girl stopped nodding. "No."

"Ask directions?"

The girl now took to shaking her head. No, they didn't get gas, they didn't ask directions. The girl seemed simultaneously certain of these facts and yet bewildered by them.

"Okay." said Garry. "Thanks."

He left the little shack and headed back to the car, surveying the lay of the land. It was due south, then, because there was nothing for as far as the eye could see except a few barns and this gas station with a broken down sedan with two flat tires. Garry slid into the saloon, so habituated to the synchronized movement of the other Garry getting into the passenger seat that he didn't initially notice that anything was out of the ordinary.

And yet there most certainly was. There was a man in the passenger seat now, and he had a shotgun.

"I'm sorry to have to do this friend." said Eddie. "But I'm kind of stuck, and I really need a ride."

Garry put his hands about shoulder high. "You want me to get out?"

"Soon enough." said Eddie. "In the meantime let's drive for a bit. What's your name?"

"Garry."

"California?"

"LA."

"What brings you to Nevada Garry?"

"Blackjack. I'm heading to Vegas."

"What's wrong with Reno? It's a lot closer."

"Tried Reno. Didn't have a lot of luck in the casinos in Reno. Lost pretty big."

Chapter 13

The sun was slipping behind the mountains and the desert was turning blue for the night. It remained hot, though, and Ray and Angel and Tim kept the top down and the speed up and they stayed on the 395, so they were back in California.

"You realize we're back in California." said Tim. He yelled now, so that he could hear himself, and it hurt.

"I know it." said Ray. "It's fine. We can head back into Nevada on the 190."

"It's pretty much a quarry trail, you know. There's nothing from Death Valley to the Nevada line but rocks."

"Exactly. No cars, no cops."

"Fine. Whatever. The 190 it is."

When they turned onto the 190 it was fully night and the moon was high and full and lighting up the desert like a cloudy day. The high-contrast effect on the rocky terrain was like a movie set that could very convincingly have staged the lunar landings. The rocks were white and colorless where the moonlight could reach them, turning sharply black where it couldn't. Tim didn't need the lights to see the road ahead, and it was hours since they'd seen another car.

"Hey, what do you say we pull off the road for a while?" said Ray.

"Are you nuts?" said Tim. "No. We're never stopping again."

"Tim, you see that sort of gateway ahead formed by two boulders? Take a left off the road just after that."

"Again, negative. We're not stopping until we need gas or we smell tortillas."

Out of the corner of his right eye Tim could see Angel getting excited about something. She put Baby to her cheek, and was telling it something important.

"Why do you want to stop?" said Tim.

"You haven't guessed?"

"No." said Tim. "Oh. Yeah. Yes, I've guessed. The haul. This is where it's buried. You knew — you've known since San Francisco — that we were going to be driving along the 190 tonight."

"Just after that boulder Tim."

Tim pulled to a stop in the dirt, to the left of a boulder so big that it hid the entire car from any traffic that might have approached from the same direction. The back tires sunk deeply into the loose gravel that stood in for ground.

"Look." said Tim, "I've got another proposition — let's keep going, get safe, lay low. When the heat's off you and Angel can come back here, without me to take a share, and you can dig it up with all the time that you need. We've got that knife nut and this Socorro guy on our trail, not to mention the cops and God knows who else. I wouldn't be surprised to see the Lone Ranger at this point."

"We're too close now, Tim." said Ray, "But what's more, so are they. They're going to figure out that we took the 190 back to Nevada so, yeah, they're going to be close on our heels. But that also means that they're as close now as they've ever been to the haul. We leave it here now we risk having nothing to come back for."

Tim let his head fall against the steering wheel.

"Tim." said Ray. "Do you know how much money we're talking about?"

"No, Ray. I don't."

"Neither do I Tim. You know why? Because there was so much we couldn't carry it all. There was so much we never got all the way through counting it. Tim just invest this little bit more time and you'll never have to do anything like this ever again."

Tim put the car back in gear and kicked some gravel on to the road. He creeped the car slowly further and further away from the highway and through an increasingly complex maze of boulders and dunes, some gentle, some treacherous. The maze cleared again and the desert opened up before them.

"Right here." said Ray. "Stop here."

They got out of the car.

"Are we looking for a big X or something?" said Tim.

"No. Over here." Ray led them toward the open desert.

Tim didn't see it until he was almost stepping into a deep, dry gorge. About sixty feet down and rocky.

"Invisible until you're almost on top of it. An illusion created by the desert." said Ray. They peered over the edge. At the bottom, almost imperceptible from the surrounding rocks under a layer of dust, was a minivan, which had clearly once been on the top of the gorge.

"Is that it?"

Ray offered only a look of withering irony.

"Now what?" said Tim.

"Now we go down and get it. Or, if you don't mind, you do."

"My head is still ringing and I've got nine fingers. Why don't you do it?"

"You want to stay up here with Angel?"

"Both of you go."

"No offense, Tim, I'm not a hundred percent convinced you'd still be here when we got back."

Tim couldn't persuasively claim that wasn't true, because it wasn't. He started making his way clumsily down the incline.

The back of the van indicated it had been new when it went over the edge. The layers of dust were impenetrable, and they'd preserved the car. The front was folded like an accordion and the van was partially buried nose first in the rocks. Tim couldn't see through the windows, so he slid open the side door.

There was a driver, a passenger, and a third corpse in the back. They were wearing their seat-belts. They had decayed with their ecosystem and were clean bones, tightly covered in a thin, cracking leather and wearing identical suits. There was nothing else in the van.

Chapter 14

"This'll do." said Eddie. They were firmly in Death Valley now, with mountains on either side, black against the night sky.

"Listen, Mister..." started Garry.

"I'm not going to kill you." said Eddie. "I just need your car and I don't need you and I even more don't need you calling the cops any time soon, but there's no one around for miles and even if someone comes along there's no phone coverage for miles, too, so I think it's safe to leave you here. Fair enough?"

"Fair enough." Garry had performed the improbable charade of a helpless victim for hours now, and he knew that he only need keep his mouth shut for another fifteen seconds. He got out of the car and made a point of walking around behind it, his hands raised, while Eddie slid into the driver's seat.

Garry stood on the road and watched as the saloon pulled away. He smelled the wind, he squared his shoulders, he estimated the speed of the car and when it was steady he drew his gun and put a bullet through the back window. He stood and watched. The saloon continued in an unwavering line, and eventually disappeared over the horizon.

Garry holstered his gun and started to walk, south, when the burst of a police siren caused him to turn to see Larry pulling to a stop behind him.

Chapter 15

"There's nothing here Ray." Tim called up the hill.

"Keep looking Tim."

"Ray, it's gone. There are no millions of dollars in this car."

"What is there then?"

"Three guys. You want me to ask them what they did with it?"

"What else?"

Tim climbed inside the van. The back was empty but for a lockbox, roughly the size of a safety deposit box, and four hand-held sub-machine guns. Tim considered the potential applications of the guns, and judged taking the hill with an Uzi as among those battles he couldn't win. Inspired, though, by the near certitude that Angel and Ray were going to leave him here at the bottom of the gorge with his new, dusty friends, he searched the corpse in the back. In the right front jacket pocket was a tiny purse .22. Tim slipped it in his pocket.

"Just a box."

"That's it. Bring it up."

"It's just a box. Like a bank deposit box."

"Bring it up Tim."

It took Tim appreciably longer to climb back up than it had taken him to get down. He dragged the box away from the edge.

"Ray, what's in here. This is not more money than you could carry or count."

"No. It's better than money." said Ray.

"What is it Honey?" asked Angel. "Moon rocks?"

"It's diamonds, Ray, isn't it?"

"No, it's not diamonds either."

"A Monet?"

"Closer. We have to go now."

"Well, we have to see it first." said Angel. "Don't we Baby?"

"If you like. Got a crowbar?"

Tim got the crowbar out of the trunk of the Cadillac. He put his foot on top of the box and the long end of the crowbar into the loop of the lock and leaned back, popping the lock off and falling backwards. Angel knelt before the box, as though at an altar, as though about to receive divine benediction. She opened the box and unfolded something covering the contents.

"What?" said Angel. "What the hell is this Ray?"

Chapter 17

Quick reflexes and a hard head and an imaginative approach to personal security are characteristics that will serve you well and even keep you alive as both cop and convict, but they're a completely different skill-set to that which is required for a desert manhunt. Eddie had been fighting and running and being kicked in the groin for 24 hours now and his otherwise admirable single-minded sense of purpose meant that he so far hadn't slept or eaten or consumed anywhere near enough fluids for a Chicago cop in Death Valley.

And he'd misjudged another critical measure, too. In the middle of the night, in the middle of Death Valley, Eddie ran out of gas. He was fatigued to the point of collapse, he was sweating away essential fluids and he could feel that his back was soaked and stuck to the car seat, and now he was out of gas.

He stayed in the car for a minute, bewildered — he had never been so far out of his element, so unprepared, so out of options. It was novel. It was, in fact, hilarious. Eddie laughed. And the more he laughed the more funny things he thought of. The poor, sad ex-heavyweight with the graft glued into his walls, the coke-addled deputy, the way — and he was just realizing this now — the way the real Ray Costa played him at the motel, the fact that he'd driven three hundred miles with a guy with a gun, and he hadn't thought to search him. It was all just too much, and now it was going to end, with a sputter, in the desert.

Eddie got out of the car and stepped out onto freshly strewn gravel. It had come from two deep treads in the loose ground at the side of the road, next to a big boulder that, with a similar boulder on the other side of the road, formed a sort of a gateway.

Larry leaned into his steering wheel, willing the car to go faster. The thug in the back seat had described Eddie, there could be no doubt, and he was only minutes behind the man who killed his son-in-law, his little girl's only hope for happiness, his deputy. Garry was handcuffed in the back, looking very much at home in the back of a police car but nevertheless alone, as though his picture was incomplete. He was happy to be along for the ride, even in handcuffs, because he, too, had a score to settle at the end of it.

Steve slowed down at the turnoff from 395 to 190. He knew that's where he was going, and there was no need to slow down, but the sign "Death Valley 101" appealed to him. He was no academic — the opposite if anything — but he felt that if he was ever going to take or maybe teach a university course it would be called something like "Death Valley 101". He banked hard and got up to speed again in seconds and in a moment he was on what looked like a straight-away all the way to the Inyo Mountains.

Chapter 18

"How is this — whatever the hell this is — how is this better than money?" asked Angel.

"Do you trust me Angel?"

Angel let the cache slip back into the box and sat up on her knees and looked an uncharacteristic firmness at Ray that said that the Angel who trusted Ray had, for the moment, left the building.

"What the hell's going on here Ray?"

"Angel, that doesn't just get us money, it gets us freedom. We're not going to Mexico. We were never going to Mexico, because we don't have to."

"You want to explain how."

"Can't. You're going to have to trust me."

"Trust you, Ray?" said Angel.

"Fraid so. Just a little longer."

"And why should I trust you, Ray?"

"Soul mates, remember?"

"No, Ray. For two years now I've been displaying advanced symptoms of schizotypal personality disorder with obsessive tendencies. I've been introducing them slowly and convincingly, so that you might believe the otherwise insane idea that I was falling in love with you. I worked for your trust, Ray, I worked hard for it. So don't just be asking me to trust you on this, just like that, 'cause I've got a lot riding on it."

Angel — probably just Angela now — stood up and raised and steadied Baby — probably just a gun now.

"Where's the money Ray?"

"There's no money Angel. I mean, there was, it was an armored car — maybe three thousand in small bills and coins. I bought beer."

"You forget, Ray, I've got your number. I know you better than you know you. Probably a lot better. And I know that the only true thing about Ray Costa is that whatever he's saying, it's a lie. A clever, meticulously detailed lie, with all the inconsistencies ironed out even as it's being spun. The key to the Ray Costa fiction is the grain of truth, and the key to that is always this — how does this lie serve the purposes of Ray Costa."

"Well, that's all true. What can I say? In this one, rare case, the truth happens to suit the situation best." And with that Angel fired Baby and the 44 mm chunk of lead cracked the bone in Ray's thigh and swept the leg out from under him. He hit the ground as though he'd been falling for miles and gave immediate voice to his pain.

"Where's the money Ray?" Angel asked again, and just as she did another shot rang out and a thousand pellets of buckshot entered her abdomen. She staggered toward the edge of the gorge, and fell off.

"You're welcome." said Eddie. He walked nearer the gorge and peered over. "Yeah. She's dead."

He gave the box a little kick. "This it?"

"Yeah." said Ray. He was making a tourniquet out of his sleeve. "I need a doctor."

"Nah." said Eddie. "You don't." He turned to Tim and smiled.

"Hi Tim." he said.

"Hi." Tim said, and gave in to his better instincts. He pulled the little .22 from his pocket, pointed, and pulled the trigger. There was a gritty, grinding resistance, and nothing else. The gun was jammed full of sand, and had been useless for years.

Eddie and Tim looked at each other, pointing their guns at each other. Then Eddie pitched forward like a felled tree. His back — from his head to his heels — was covered in blood, and a significant portion of the back of his head was missing, and had been since Garry took that crack shot on the highway.

"Get me to the car Tim." said Ray.

"Why, Ray? Why would I want to spend another second with you? You know, Ray, I thought my life was going pretty bad until I met you, but I had no idea, did I? Just how much carnage a real professional could bring. So, thanks for that, I guess. You've given me a real appreciation for the relatively non-fatal, ten-fingered, full auditory experience that I was living before I heard the name Ray Costa."

"Because of the box, Tim, that's why. It's no good to you, you have to know what to do with it.

"The box? I'm sure that's true. I'm sure it's some complex and dangerous mystery that I wouldn't grasp and, in fact, I already don't understand ninety percent of what's happened to me today, but I know one thing for sure — I want nothing to do with whatever is in that box."

"Yeah, you do Tim. Trust me."

"Trust you? Are you seriously asking me to trust you? Seriously?"

"No, Tim, you're right, you got me. This whole thing was an elaborate ruse to trick you into driving me to the hospital from the middle of the desert. I've been shot, Tim, this is my serious voice."

Tim picked up the box and put it under his right arm. He offered Ray his hand and pulled him to his feet and wrapped Ray's arm over his shoulder. They hobbled toward the neon pink Coupe de Ville and arrived at it just as Sheriff Larry LaLande pulled out of the stone maze that hid them from the road.

Larry rolled up with his gun already in hand and held out the window, trained on Ray and Tim.

"I can't believe this." said Tim. "I'm seriously, and I mean seriously, starting to doubt that this is actually happening."

"Just stay right where you are." said Larry. He got out of his car. "Now, where's that big fella with the knife fetish?"

"We got no idea Sheriff." said Ray, before Tim could make what Ray considered the fundamental mistake of giving away real information that you didn't have to. "I've been shot."

"You don't say." said Larry. "Which one of you fellas is Ray Costa?"

Ray glanced up at Tim. "I am." he said.

"That it?" said Larry, gesturing with his gun toward the box.

"Yeah." said Ray.

"All right then." Larry opened the back door of the car and ordered Garry out.

"You." he said to Ray. "In."

Ray limped the rest of the way by himself and lay down in the back of the police car. Larry closed him in. He unlocked Garry's cuffs and sent him over to stand with Tim. He appraised the comparison.

"A little unequal, maybe, but it should sell. Open the box."

Garry took the box from Tim and put it on the ground and opened it. He unfolded the material covering the contents, as Angel had done, and looked every bit as shocked and surprised as she had.

"What is it?" asked Larry. Garry didn't look up. Or blink. Or, by outward appearance, breathe. Larry took Ike Sugar's gym back out of his car through the window. "Here." he said, throwing the bag to Garry from a safe distance. "Put that in the box instead."

Garry had already twigged and now Tim did, too. The sheriff was staging a tragic standoff — two desperadoes in the desert, shooting each other over a few thousand dollars in what appeared to be, from Tim's perspective, a papier maché globe. Garry didn't respond. He concentrated on keeping his eyebrows as high on his forehead as he could manage.

"Oh, hell, now what?" said Larry, as the a baritone revolutions of a Harley Davidson began echoing gently off the rocks. Steve rolled to a stop behind the police car. He dismounted and stood by his bike, removing his gloves.

"What are you supposed to be dressed as?" asked Larry.

Steve took Pipo from the saddle bags. He wasn't looking at Larry. He showed no sign of so much as noticing Larry. Or Tim for that matter. He walked to his henchman.

"Boss, I..." Garry started with no clear idea how to finish. He stood, slowly, still looking every bit as scandalized as when he first laid eyes on the contents of the box.

"You shouldn'a look in the box, Garry." Steve backhanded Pipo on a swift arc, connecting with Garry's jaw and lifting him briefly off the ground. He lay where he fell. He breathed slowly. His arm twitched. Steve raised Pipo over his head and brought it down again on Garry's. Pipo clanged on the stones beneath Garry's head.

Steve turned and looked at Tim, who only just managed to look back. Steve looked right into his soul and saw, apparently, someone with no interest in the contents of the box. He ignored Tim.

"Where is Ray Costa?" Steve asked the sheriff.

Larry had a very rapid internal debate. The suppositions were as follows: 1. This huge gang-banger was unarmed. 2. Except for the pipe and it, clearly, counts. 3. He wants Ray Costa. 4. Ray Costa would be useful to Larry in explaining and excusing his recent activities. 5. There's probably no staging a convincing shootout now. 6. Living through this should probably be given higher priority.

"He's in my car." said Larry.

"Take him back to prison, Sheriff." said Steve. "Is where he belongs."

Larry appeared to run another internal debate but the suppositions were much more limited and so it was only a few seconds before the fog cleared and he got into his car.

"That your ride?" Steve said to Tim.

"Yeah. Sort of."

"Sweet car."

"Thanks."

"You look in the box?"

"No."

"Did anyone else look in the box?"

"Angel. Angel looked in the box."

"Who's Angel?"

"She's dead. That knife guy shot her and she went over the gorge?"

"What knife guy? What gorge?"

"Over there. They're kind of hard to see, but there's a gorge. And a guy with a hole in the back of his head."

Steve picked his way over the desert terrain of invisible gorges with the measured disdain of a cat crossing a damp lawn.

"Did he look in the box?" Steve asked Tim.

"He's dead. No, he didn't, but he's dead."

"No he ain't." said Steve. He nudged Eddie with Pipo. Then he nudged him again. Eddie rolled onto his back and, without looking up at Steve, he shot him in the face with the shotgun.

The remains of Steve stood balanced as though by an invisible string, and then collapsed in on themselves like a an imploded apartment block.

Eddie stood, or tried to, and made it to one knee. "Who was that?"

"You don't even know who it was and you killed him?"

"I thought he was going to kill me."

"I wish he had, you psycho." said Tim.

This entire scene had played out for Larry, behind the wheel of his car, as surreal theater, and all he understood of it was that the man who sliced open his deputy's throat and left him to bleed to death on a filthy motel room floor was right in front him. Larry put his car in gear and stepped on the gas. He was going about 30 when he hit Eddie, far too fast to stop in time, even if he had seen the gorge, which he didn't. Eddie, Larry and Ray went over the edge and to the bottom of the gorge. They landed right next to and with very much the same disposition as the minivan.

Chapter 19

Tim was in Utah before he realized that he never looked in the box, and he didn't regret it in the slightest. Whatever it was, it had almost certainly been rendered valueless and, if possible, even more dangerous by the events of the last 24 hours. And anyway he had a sweet pink Cadillac Coupe de Ville and what must have been over $15,000 in a slowly hardening ball of paper and paste from which he was able to peel tens and twenties as he needed them on the road. More than enough to get to New York or New Jersey and get installed there, in some affordable but clean, self-contained apartment with hot water and an address that he could put on job applications.

It began to rain. Then it began to rain hard. The thundering beat on the canvas roof of the Cadillac and the smell of wet corn made him laugh out loud with the full, surround-sound experience of not being in California. He put the heat on and it didn't work. If anything it got colder in the car. The roof didn't seal very well, either, and rain-water started to drip in, run down the windshield onto the rear view mirror, and eventually catch a current of wind to become a recurring spray of refrigerant in Tim's face.

New York was not the place to get top dollar for a neon pink Cadillac convertible, especially when selling it for cash. This was more of a Florida car. Miami, in fact. And Miami's as good as anywhere. Better, even, because it's not San Francisco but it's got a similar, Latin, multi-layered dynamic. The sort of environment in which a guy like Tim — with a clean slate and a decent stake and a willingness to do what it takes — could thrive.

When he got to where the 180 crashes into Salt Lake City and a man has to make a decision, Tim got onto the 15, heading south.

THE DEER WOMAN

COURTNEY VAUGHN

The grass on the prairie swayed in the wind as the guineas clucked and plucked ticks from the dry, cracked earth. Pigs snorted into their slop trough and squealed as they rooted one another aside, trying to fill their bellies. Their ears twitched as the flies tried to rest on them. The tiny black wings and feet tickled wherever they landed. Beads of perspiration caught in Sarah's eyelashes and stung her eyes. She wiped her forehead with her arm. Dust turned to mud in the streams of her sweat.

She picked up the bucket that she had balanced on the knotty fence. The smell of the pigs was as familiar to her as the wrinkles on her calloused hands. In the distance, thunder faintly rumbled. Sarah shielded her eyes with her hand and peered into the distance. Hopefully the rain would make it to them this time. The crops were parched, and the well was low. The wooden bucket banged against her hip as she lugged it back to the house. The rough, rope handle sawed against her palm.

Jacob's weather-worn boots were on the front porch. They had a hole in the bottom of the soul, but even so they were his better pair of shoes. The wooden slats creaked under her weight as she pulled open the door. It drooped in a lopsided fashion that left a small gap at the top even when it was closed. The bottom corner had grated against the porch until an arc was scarred into the slats, marking its path. Sarah's eyes took a moment to adjust to the dimness of their little home.

In the far right corner she could make out their bed. It was draped with a threadbare, patchwork quilt that Jacob's mother had given them as a wedding present ten years ago. The other side of the house had a wobbly table Jacob had handcrafted for them. His hands were better suited to praying than they were to manual labor. Three stools sat beside the table. Two of them were well worn and smooth from years of sitting. The third one was just as rough as the day it was made. Jacob had made it for their future child, but they had not been blessed with that yet. Looking at the stool made Sarah ache inside, but putting it away would feel like giving up.

Sarah placed the bucket by the fireplace. The hearth was made from river stones that the Heely boys had dug out for them in exchange for helping their ma through childbirth. Money was sparse, so people did what they could for one another. Mostly manual labor or a few ears of corn were used for payment of services. Sarah ran the edge of her hand across the table to scrape away crumbs from breakfast. She caught them in her other hand and dusted them into the slop bucket. Her white apron was tinged brown with sweat stains and dirt. She lifted the hem to wipe off her face as she heard hooves clopping against the ground outside. She straightened her apron and headed back out into the sun's heat.

The Doc was waiting for her in the yard as the wooden door fell shut against the door frame behind her. "Hello, Mrs. Cartwright. You ready?" A gray mare was following behind the buckskin he was riding.

"Afternoon, Doc." She took the reins to the mare from his outstretched hand and placed her left foot in the stirrup before swinging herself up into the saddle. "Alright, let's go." Sarah patted the side of Maggie's neck as she urged the horse to follow Doc further into the prairie. Her gait was steady as they plodded across the ground.

Sarah helped Doc Brannigan from time to time with births and minor wounds. When the town was as small as Fort Marshall, people had to lend a hand when they could just to make due. Today she and Doc were heading over to the Indian camp just past Hindman's Ridge. The Kiowa allowed Doc and herself to barter for medicinal herbs. Doc had helped the chief's daughter when she was attacked by a bear. He had found her bleeding on the plains and had patched her up. The braves found him tending to her and brought them both back to the tribe. When the girl had survived her wounds, Chief Two Crows had allowed Doc to live, and as part of his appreciation offered access to their medicines.

Buzzards circled off to the right as they rode. Another wave of thunder rumbled in the distance. Maggie's ears twitched as she listened to the thunder roll over the sounds of the crickets in the grass. A breeze bowed the tall grass of the plains and played with flyaway hairs that framed Sarah's face. Doc straightened himself in his saddle. Riding was becoming more of an issue for him as he got older.

"Doing ok, Doc?"

"It's just the weather. Wreaks havoc on my joints." His graying hair feathered around his head in the wind.

"Do we need to take a break?" Sarah's worry lines furrowed as she looked at him.

Doc shook his head and smiled through the pain, "No, we need to get this done before the storm hits." He always put the wellbeing of others before his own. The Reagan baby had a case of cholera. The Kiowa had chokecherry bark and few other things Doc needed.

It was about an hour before the tribe came into view. Sarah could see the smoke from their fires before she could see the teepees. As they got closer, she could see the people moving about. Half-naked children ran around the camp chasing one another. Braves fashioned arrows and spears. Squaws tended to meat cooking over a fire and shucked corn. A few of the children called out in trilling noises as the two riders approached. Pale Sparrow emerged from a flap in a deerskin teepee and greeted them. She had been found by the Kiowa when she was eight. Her blonde hair was in a plated braid over her shoulder. Her family had been killed in a shootout. She was the only survivor. Pale Sparrow had learned their language and had managed to keep most of her own as well. She served as the translator for their meetings.

Doc eased himself out of his saddle and handed his reins to a young boy who had run up to them eagerly. Doc pulled a bundle out of his saddle bag and secured it under his arm. He tousled the boy's dark hair as he walked past him to Pale Sparrow who greeted them with a smile. Sarah slid off of Maggie and handed her horse's reins to the boy as well.

The horses followed him willingly to a wooden post where he tied them up. She longingly watched the boy and a few other children run off to play while Pale Sparrow and Doc greeted one another.

"Blessings." Pale Sparrow held the doctor's hand in hers and embraced Sarah warmly as she broke out of her trance and joined them.

"Blessings," Doc gestured to the goods under his arm, "I need to see Wandering Coyote."

Pale Sparrow bowed her head and lifted the flap in the teepee she had emerged from earlier. Sarah followed Doc into the hide structure. It smelled like tobacco and nutmeg inside. Wandering Coyote was sitting cross legged in front of a small fire. The warmth was almost sweltering. He wore a bear's claw around his neck on a leather chord. Feathers decorated small braids in his long, dark hair. His skin was wrinkled, and one eye was clouded over. He gestured for them to sit with him.

Doc unrolled the bundle he had carried with him. He had brought some corn whiskey, some metal spoons, and a steel knife. Wandering Coyote picked up each item in his hands and looked them over. He turned his gaze to Pale Sparrow and nodded.

"What do you need today?" Behind her were leather pouches stuffed with dried herbs and bits of roots.

"Chokecherry bark, blackberry root, and wild ginger." Doc wiped sweat away from his eyes while she loaded a pouch with what they needed. She also gave them a few more things that Sarah didn't recognize. Once the pouch was full, Pale Sparrow handed it to Doc. She followed them back outside as they headed for their horses. The blonde woman took Sarah's arm and pulled her aside as Doc tucked the medicine into this saddle bag.

"I saw you looking at the children." Pale Sparrow handed Sarah a small pouch of her own. "This is red clover. Boil the leaves and drink the tea from it. It will help with fertility."

Sarah was taken aback. Her eyes brimmed with tears of gratitude as she closed her hand on the pouch of herbs. She hugged Pale Sparrow tightly and whispered in her ear, "Thank you." She clutched the small leather satchel in her hand as she climbed back on Maggie's bony back.

The wind was picking up now. Doc urged his horse to gallop faster. Maggie lagged behind. Her age made it harder for her to keep up. Her breath felt labored under Sarah's weight. Tiny water droplets splattered on Sarah's hands and trickled through her hair to her scalp. The coldness of the rain awakened goosebumps on her arms.

Jacob was waiting on the porch when they arrived back at the Cartwright's home. He rushed out into the rain to hold Maggie still as his wife climbed out of the saddle. He handed the reins to Doc. The two men tilted their heads to one another, and Doc trotted off in the direction of the rest of the town. Rain started to pelt harder on the ground, turning the parched dirt to mud.

Sarah let out a sigh of relief as she pulled off her wet clothes and laid them in front the fire Jacob had built. She tucked the pouch with the red clover under her wet apron so Jacob wouldn't see it. The burning wood hissed as a few drops of rain found their way down the chimney. "How is Mr. Gains doing?"

"He's near the end." Jacob had sat with the family as they prayed over the old man. There was nothing left that Doc could do for him, so as the town preacher it was time for Jacob to step in. Mr. Gains' time had run its course. "He has maybe a few days left. A week at the most."

Jacob watched his wife as she pulled a night dress on. She was still as beautiful as the day he had married her. Sarah pulled a few potatoes from a sack and started peeling them. Jacob walked up behind her and encircled her waist in his arms. He held her close and swayed back and forth with her.

"You're going to make me cut myself." Sarah laughed as she held the knife in one hand and the potato in the other. She turned her head to kiss her husband. His dark whiskers scratched at her cheek.

"What do you need me to do?" Jacob let her go after the kiss and pushed up his sleeves. He shook his black hair out of his eyes.

"Could you fill the pot with some water and hang it by the fire to boil?" Sarah used the knife in her hand to point to a black pot with a metal handle sitting by the hearth.

Jacob picked up a ladle from their water bucket and dropped a few scoops into the pot before hanging it by the handle on the hook above the fire. He repositioned one of the stools so that he could sit across from her while she cooked. He lifted his worn bible from the corner of the table and picked it up to read to her. "Deuteronomy, chapter thirty-one, verse eight: And the Lord, He is the One who goes before you. He will be with you; He will not leave you nor forsake you; do not fear nor be dismayed."

In all the years of being a preacher's wife, Sarah never got tired of hearing her husband read scriptures to her. His voice was kind and loving. The pages of his bible were thin and faded from years of use. Corners were bent to mark his favorite verses. Her knife chopped rhythmically as he read. She carried the potatoes to the pot and dumped them in. The water was barely starting to bubble. She chopped up a carrot and an onion and added them as well. Flour sprinkled from her hand into the pot as she thickened the soup. A dash of salt and pepper floated on top of the broth as she stirred everything in.

Thunder shook the house. Outside, the pigs squealed in terror as lightening carved its way across the sky. Sarah sipped the broth. It still tasted mostly like water, but it was the best she could do with what they had right now. The next coach with a delivery for the General Store was still a few weeks away, and Mr. and Mrs. Harper were already low on everything.

Once the potatoes and carrots were soft, Sarah ladled some of the soup into a bowl and placed it on the table in front of her husband. He smiled at her gratefully and pulled it closer to him as she filled her own bowl and joined him at the table.

Jacob reached out for Sarah's hands, and they both bowed their heads. Fire light reflected off of their faces as Jacob began saying grace, "Father God, we thank you for this meal we are about to eat and ask that you let it nourish our bodies. We ask that you please be with Mr. Gains and his family and help them through the days to come. We ask that if it is your will, that we be blessed with a child, and that you help us to always follow your path. Thank you for the rain and for Sarah and the Doc's safe journey today. I ask that you speak through me this Sunday as I give my sermon, and in your name we pray, amen."

"Amen," Sarah echoed softly after him. She sipped her soup, but her mind kept wandering to the herbs stashed under her apron. She was worried that if Jacob knew about them he would think she was taking the pregnancy into her own hands and out of God's. Maybe God wanted Pale Sparrow to give her the herbs. Maybe this was His way of helping her when even her own body seemed against her. It was one thing to use herbs as medicine for a cold, but to use them in the hopes of conceiving a child felt almost like witchcraft. Sarah chewed a piece of potato slowly as she thought about the decision she would have to make.

"Are you ok?" Jacob sat down his bowl and touched her hand lightly. "You look worried and far away."

His words brought her out of her thoughts, and she smiled at him reassuringly, "Yes, I'm fine. Just worried about the Doc." Sarah tilted her head down as she looked into her bowl, "His arthritis is getting bad, and this weather always makes it worse."

"Well, we can go look in on him in the morning. Would that make you feel better?" He ran his thumb over the back of her hand.

Sarah wove her fingers between his and nodded, "Yes."

Outside, horses whinnied in distress between thunderclaps, and a loud unnatural crack echoed. Jacob stood up from the table. His stool clattered to the floor behind him as he rushed to the door. Sarah's heartbeat thudded against her ribcage. Her husband's figure was silhouetted in the doorframe as lightening arched across the sky.

"What is it?" Sarah found herself on her feet. Her voice was lost in the next rumble of thunder.

Jacob ran into the yard. The door slammed shut behind him. Sarah's bare feet padded against the floor as she raced to see what was going on. Her hand flung open the door. Through the curtain of rain, she saw Jacob hunched over a heap in their yard. Another flash of lightening revealed a stagecoach that was tilted on its side. One wheel was spinning in the air. Rain bounced off of the body of the wagon and into the already forming puddles. Jacob climbed on top of the wagon and jerked the door open. Sarah saw the top half of his body reach into the coach. She was standing on the porch. A small puddle of water gathered in a dip in the wood. Jacob's head emerged from the wreckage. Something was cradled in his arms.

"Sarah!" He yelled out over the storm.

Sarah's feet splashed across the porch. Cold mud squelched between her toes. She stood on her tiptoes as Jacob leaned over and handed her the bundle in his arms. As her arms cradled it, she could feel the slight movement of tiny hands and feet. It was a baby swaddled in a dark blanket. A cry erupted from the bundle as the child squirmed in her arms. Rain was soaking into the blanket. Sarah looked back up at her husband. He was trying to lift another man out of the coach. Jacob managed to get the man's arm looped over his shoulder as he struggled to get leverage. His boots slid on the wet wood as he tried to brace both himself and the added body weight of the other man. Sarah noticed that the coach's passenger was offering no help at all. His body was completely limp as Jacob fought to get them both back onto the ground safely.

Bracing the child against her chest, Sarah padded back up onto the porch and over to the door. She held it open as her husband towed the stranger across the lawn. The toes of the man's boots drug across the ground, leaving behind a trail in the mud. Jacob laid the man down on the floor in front of the fire. He wadded up Sarah's clothing that she had laid there to dry earlier and tucked them under the man's head as a make shift pillow. Sarah held the whimpering child up to her shoulder and rocked it gently while she watched her husband lower his ear to the man's mouth and then his chest. Jacob couldn't feel any breath coming from the man's nose or mouth, and he couldn't hear any heartbeat.

"Stay here!" Jacob pointed his finger sternly at his wife as he ran back out into the night.

Sarah paced nervously near the bed trying to calm the baby, "Shhh. You're ok. It's ok." Her body bounced lightly with each step. The rhythmic jostling soothed him. "It's ok, little one." Slowly the child's crying stopped. "There. See? You're ok. You're ok, baby."

The door flung open, startling Sarah. Her heart flew into her throat as she looked into the darkness. Doc stepped across the threshold followed by Jacob. Both of them were drenched from the raging storm.

"Over by the fire." Jacob jerked his head towards the man's unconscious body.

Doc knelt by the man's head and kneaded his neck with his fingers trying to find a pulse. The fire flickered and sputtered as the rain continued to find its way down the chimney. Doc shook his head and started doing chest compressions, occasionally pausing to blow into the man's mouth. After a few moments he paused, "He's gone. Most likely killed in the crash." Doc stood up, bracing his back with his hands. The joints in his knees groaned and popped as he stood up. He motioned towards Sarah with his hands, urging her closer, "Let's take a look at the little one."

Sarah carried the baby over to Doc and folded her arms anxiously over her chest, "What'll happen to it now?"

"Well first," Doc laid the baby on the table and unwrapped the blanket, "let's make sure it's healthy."

The baby looked less than a year old. Under the blanket, the child was naked except for a cloth diaper that was pinned on its bottom. It had a tuft of dark hair on its tiny head, and blue eyes looked up at them. Doc unpinned the diaper that was wrapped around it. As the cloth was pulled back, they saw it was a baby boy. He kicked his legs trying to wriggle away. Doc looked him over from head to toe checking for any sign of trauma or bruising.

"He looks healthy enough. No sign of swelling or any bruises." He pinned the diaper back on the baby. Sarah brought him a dry strip of cloth to wrap the child in so the blanket could dry. "In the morning we can send word to a few of the towns nearby to see if anyone knows about a man and a baby on a stagecoach. Any luck, someone will know who they are."

"What about tonight?" Jacob was staring at the man lying in their floor.

"If you can help me get him on my horse, I can take the body to the undertaker's for storage. Maybe drop the baby off with the school teacher?"

Sarah scooped up the baby, "There's no need to bother Miss Adams at this time of night. We can watch over him."

Doc turned to look at Sarah with solemn, understanding eyes, "Well, alright then. I'll drop by in the morning with some milk for him." He nodded to Jacob who grabbed the man's boots as Doc bent down with a groan to grab his shoulders.

The two men hobbled outside with the body, leaving Sarah alone with the baby. "Sweet, sweet baby." She cooed over him and he nestled his head in the curve of her neck. Sarah felt an overwhelming wave of love and appreciation. Her eyes flitted up towards heaven as her lips quivered into a smile. The baby's soft breath pulsed into her throat. A whisper escaped from her, "Thank you." She felt more blessed in that moment than she had in her entire life.

Jacob came back in the house and sloughed off his soaked boots. Tiny clods of mud tumbled off of their soles as he sat them by the door. He slowly approached his wife who was swaying slightly from side to side with the baby cuddled up next to her. He noticed small tears trickling down her cheeks, "Hey, are you ok?" Jacob cupped her face gently in his hands.

Sarah nodded with a small laugh, "Yes, I'm wonderful." Her eyes sparkled in the firelight. "Jake, what if this is God's way of giving us a baby?" Her voice was hesitant as she searched his face for a reaction. She bit her bottom lip as her face beamed with hope and joy.

"Sarah, this child could have a mother out there somewhere who is missing him terribly...we can't keep him." Jacob's eyes were full of sadness as he stroked her cheek with his thumb.

"If we can't find his family, he will need someone to take care of him." Sarah clutched the baby closer to her body, "Why can't that be us?"

Jacob sighed and rubbed his temples. He paced the length of the room as he thought about how to handle the situation. He had wanted a child as badly as his wife had, and they had tried for years. He faced her once more. Her hope was tangible in the air around them. "Ok," Jacob's voice was tentative, "if we make an honest effort to find his family, and no one comes forward, then we can take care of him."

"Ok." Sarah choked back laughter of elated happiness as she hugged her husband and held the baby between them. The two of them looked down at his face. "He'll need a name."

"Try not to get too attached, darling. We don't know how long we'll have him." The joy in Sarah's eyes dimmed as he spoke, "But, I guess we will have to call him something while he's here." Jacob stroked her hair.

"Gabriel." Sarah whispered over the sleeping baby in her arms.

"Gabriel." Jacob echoed as he touched the baby's head gently. He tried to fight back the joy he felt seeing his wife with a baby in her arms.

She would be heartbroken if the baby's family was found. After years of failure to conceive, Jacob didn't know if she could take that kind of heart ache. He silently prayed that the child didn't have anyone else. Part of him felt disgusted at himself for wishing such horrible things, but part of him still hoped it was true.

Sarah pulled a woven basket out of the corner of the room and filled it with scraps of cloth to create a makeshift bed for the child. She set it by the side of their bed and nestled Gabriel inside. Jacob pulled off his wet clothing and clumsily knelt beside the bed. Sarah joined him as he prayed, but she kept one hand on the basket where Gabriel was sleeping as her husband's voice quietly drifted into the night.

"Father God, we ask for your guidance with this child. We ask that if he has family, you let them hear word of his safe rescue. We ask that if he is alone in this world that you give us your blessing on raising him up to be a Godly man. We ask that you look after the soul of the man who lost his life tonight, and that you bring him and his family peace, dear Lord. Thank you for our home and this small blessing that you have brought to us, no matter how long or short that blessing may last. Please keep us on your path and guide us towards your will. In your name we pray, amen."

"Amen." Sarah turned her face towards Gabriel as the prayer finished. In her heart she felt that he was already hers.

Jacob climbed into bed and scooted himself up against the wall to make room for his wife. Sarah laid herself down beside her husband. She let one hand dangle off of the side of the bed to touch the basket. Touching his bed reassured her that it was real and not just a dream. Jacob's arm wrapped around her as they settled in. For once, she felt like her family was complete. After a few hours of gazing lovingly down at Gabriel, Sarah finally drifted off to sleep.

The sound of a rooster broke through Sarah's peaceful dreams. Gabriel whined softly in his basket. Sarah leaned over the edge of the bed and picked him up. "Hi, baby boy. Good morning." Her voice was soothing as she cradled him close to her.

Jacob stirred next to her. He propped himself up on his elbows. A sleepy smile spread across his face. He sat up and kissed Sarah on the shoulder. "Good morning."

"Hi," she whispered back lovingly.

"How is the little man doing?"

"A little fussy. He's probably hungry." Sarah shifted so that Jacob could take Gabriel from her arms.

"Doc should be back by soon." The tiny body felt so fragile in his arms. He leaned in and kissed the baby's forehead before handing him back to Sarah. "I need to get dressed. We have a lot to do today."

Sarah lifted Gabriel's basket and carried it over to the table. She laid him back down while she went about cooking breakfast. She watched Jake pull up his trousers and slip his feet into the boots he wore last night. There was a slight squelching sound as his feet pressed against the soles. His other pair of shoes were most likely still soaked from sitting on the porch all night, so he would have to make due. Sarah made a mental note to set them out in the sun later.

Thick oatmeal fell off of the wooden stirring spoon into a bowl. Sarah dusted the top of the blob with the last of their remaining sugar and passed it to Jacob. She dished herself out a small portion and sat beside the baby at the table. Jacob blew on his food and said a brief prayer to bless their day. As they ate, the sound of boots walking across the porch came through the door followed by a rapping knock.

"Come on in, Doc." Jacob's words were muffled through his food.

Doc Brannigan opened the door, "Good morning. How is my littlest patient, hmm?"

"He'll be a lot better once he's had some of that milk you're carrying." Sarah stood up as Doc handed her a bottle of milk.

"I had a spare in the cupboard. The rubber tip has seen a few teething infants, but it should still do the trick." Doc watched as Sarah picked up the baby and brought the bottle to his lips. "Oh, before I forget, here's some extra milk from the Canady's. Helen says you just come on over if you need anything." He placed a glass jug of milk on the table.

"Thank you, Doc. I'll make sure to stop by later and thank Mrs. Canady. I'm sure she'll want to see where the milk is going." Sarah watched delightedly as Gabriel took to the bottle. His blue eyes stared up at her as he fed.

"I've got Thomas sending out a telegram to Canyon City, and Luke said he had to make a ride out to Darby Ridge today, so he's taking word that way. Undertaker said he can keep the body for a week before the stench gets too bad. Maybe something will turn up." Doc ran his hand over his leathery neck. "Well, Jacob, do you have any plans for that coach outside?"

"Reckon I'll see if we can fix it. Town could use a new stagecoach."

"I think Mr. Havisham would be greatly obliged to that." Doc smiled.

Jacob finished off the rest of his oatmeal and stood up, "Let's go take a look at it." He kissed Sarah and the baby before walking outside with Doc.

Sarah watched as Gabriel's eyes slowly drifted closed. His belly was full, and he was ready to sleep again. She nestled him back into his basket and put on her dirty clothes that had dried by the fire. She would get Jake's clothes from him tonight and wash up some laundry by the creek tomorrow. The red clover fell out of its hiding place as she picked up her apron. Sarah ran her fingers over the soft leather pouch. She turned to face Gabriel. Maybe she wouldn't need the herbs after all. The floor creaked a little as she walked over to the hope chest her mother had given her on her wedding day. A thin layer of dust covered the top of the chest as she lifted the lid and sifted through the lace curtains and copper pots. She buried the small leather pouch at the bottom of the chest and shut the lid.

Outside, she could hear wood creaking and the muffled sound of the men's voices as they looked over the wagon. Sarah tidied up the kitchen and straightened the blanket on the bed. The heat of the day was already starting to seep into the small house. She picked up the basket with Gabriel in it and headed outside to gather eggs before it got much hotter.

The days wore on quickly and happily for Jacob and Sarah. Sarah hadn't stopped smiling since she had taken in Gabriel. The first few weeks were the hardest. She was always worrying if someone would come to claim him, but as time went on that fear steadily diminished. Days turned to weeks, and weeks melted into months. Gabriel was a happy addition to their family, and even though numerous telegrams had been sent, no one had come to collect the baby. The man who had died in the rainy night that Gabe came to live with them was given a nameless grave marked with a wooden cross. The child brought them so much joy, it was hard to imagine their lives without him now. Some of the other women were able to spare a few pieces of clothing that their children had out grown, and other supplies were donated as needed. Jacob had offered to build him a crib, but luckily Mr. Havisham constructed one before he could. It was a thank you gift for the stagecoach he used to transport families and goods between the towns.

The weather was beginning to cool off some. The sweat of summer no longer hung humidly in the air. The pigs were becoming lazy as the days shortened and their bodies grew plumper. Some of them would be slaughtered in a few more months to make a Christmas dinner for the town. Doc's body was becoming less and less cooperative as the colder weather moved in. He was drinking herbal teas from the Kiowa almost daily to fight the pain in his joints. There had been a few times that Sarah had to ride out to the tribe on her own to get his medicine because of how poorly he was doing. Jacob had been furious with her when he learned she had gone on her own. He said it was too dangerous for a woman to be riding alone across the prairie, especially when she was intentionally riding to an Indian camp. It had been one of the only times in their marriage that they had fought.

Sarah stood by the pig pen, dumping leftovers into the trough while Gabriel pulled at bits of weeds in the yard. He was crawling now. His hair was growing in thick and dark on top of his head. An unhappy squeal came from his tiny lungs as a worm wriggled across his chubby fingers. Sarah laughed and picked him up, knocking the worm off of him. He clung to her apron for comfort as she soothed him. Across the prairie, an unfamiliar coach jostled towards Fort Marshall. Ruts and rocks knocked against its wheels, shaking it from side to side. The horses were as black as ink. Their manes were stray pen strokes in the wind. Sarah hoisted Gabriel higher on her hip as she watched the wagon bump and jump across the grassy plains. She picked up the slop bucket with her free hand and brushed a stray hair from her face.

The coach's wood had been painted red with gold filigree. One piece of luggage was strapped to the top. As the stagecoach rumbled by, a pale woman peeled back the curtain and peered out at Sarah and the baby. Her hair was almost as red as the coach. Her stare made Sarah uneasy. The woman closed the curtain again once the wagon was passed them. Sarah's heart beat rapidly, even though she wasn't quite sure why. Gabriel picked up on the change in her mood and started to cry. Sarah rocked him gently and whispered sweetly to him as she tried to get her own emotions under control. The bucket banged against her hip as she took the baby inside.

Around dinner time, Jacob came back from helping the Heely boys learn to read. They had to spend most of their time working the farm, since their pa died. Jacob and Miss Adams took turns tutoring them so they wouldn't fall too far behind the other kids in town.

Jake slid out of his boots and scooped Gabe up from where he was playing on the floor. He plopped down on his stool while waiting for

Sarah to fix his plate like she did every night. "How was my boy today?" He looked down at Gabriel while he bounced him on his knee.

"He was an absolute angel, weren't you?" Sarah slid Jacob's plate to him and reached over the table to touch Gabe's nose with her forefinger. He giggled at her touch. "Hey, did you see that stagecoach that rolled into town this afternoon?" She tried to sound less interested than she was as she brought it up.

"Uh, yeah," Jacob was distracted with the baby, "it was someone from Bakersfield, I think."

"Why would someone from Bakersfield come all the way out here?" Sarah played with the stew in her bowl as she talked.

Jacob took a bite of his dinner and chewed contemplatively, "I think she was looking for someone. Doc is letting her stay at his place since the two rooms above the General Store are currently full. I saw them chatting on my way back."

"I hope she's not here long."

"Sarah," Jacob's spoon clattered into his bowl, "that is not the way we need to act towards strangers. We need to make them feel welcome."

Sarah tilted her head down in shame. She nodded slowly, and they finished the rest of their meal in silence.

The rooster crowed, welcoming the sun the next day. Jacob and Sarah got dressed as Gabriel dozed back to sleep. A knock trilled on the doorframe. Gabe fussed at the sound of the noise.

Jacob's boots thudded heavily as he walked to the door and opened it, "Oh hey, Doc, come on in. Where is that lodger of yours this morning?"

"Mrs. Canady is fixing her some breakfast. Actually, that's what I came to talk to you about." Doc ran his callused hands over his whiskered face, "Sarah, Jacob, I think you two should probably sit down."

Sarah's stomach dropped. Her hands shook as she took a seat. She clasped her fingers tightly in her lap trying to hide her nervous quivering, "What is it?" Her voice was a trembling whisper.

"The woman who came into town yesterday was looking for her husband and her child. The descriptions she gave match that of the man who died in the carriage and of Gabriel."

Doc's words felt like a punch in the gut to Sarah. She couldn't breathe. Her hand flew to her chest, "No. It's not true."

Jacob walked behind his wife and placed his hands on her shoulders. "How do we know she's telling the truth?"

Doc fiddled in his pocket and pulled out an oval, gold locket. He opened it and handed it to Sarah, "She also had this."

The locket had a black and white photo of the man from the wreckage on one side, and a picture of baby Gabriel on the other. Sarah's trembling hand covered her mouth as she looked at the pictures. Tears began to fall down her cheeks silently. "No, please no." She looked up at her husband pleadingly.

"Sarah, if she is his mother, we have to give him back." Jacob held her head close to him as she cried. "If he had been your child, and you had lost him—"

"He is my child!" Sarah cried out as she stood up and pulled away from her husband. She picked up the baby and held him close. The familiar warmth of his breath in the curve of her neck deepened the ache in her heart.

"I've talked to her, and she has agreed to give you the rest of the day to say your goodbyes. You'll need to bring the baby by my place around sundown." Doc had given up trying to talk to Sarah. He focused his words on Jacob now who nodded in understanding.

"Thank you, Doc." Jake handed him back the locket. He fought back his own tears as Doc Brannigan excused himself from their home. After they had sat on the bed for a moment in mournful silence, Jake spoke up with false optimism, "Let's just take today to enjoy him a little more, ok?"

Sarah was rocking gently back and forth, "I don't know if I can do it, Jake. I don't know if I can give him up."

"I'll be there with you. We can do it together." He pulled her into him, and for a moment they tried to pretend their happy little family would last forever.

Dusk came far too quickly. There were so many laughs and new discoveries that they would never get to experience together. Sarah's eyes were red and puffy from hours of crying. Gabriel tried to make her smile, but each time he did, her smile would morph back into sobs.

"It's time." Jacob helped her to her feet.

Sarah's legs were numb as she carried Gabe towards the door. She walked with Jacob towards Doc's tiny home that often doubled as his clinic. "Oh no," she turned solemnly to her husband, "we forgot his blanket. He can't sleep without it." Slight panic rang from her throat.

"It's ok. I'll go back and get it for him." Jake kissed her cheek and turned to go get the blanket.

Sarah eased up to Doc's porch trying to steel her nerves. Through the murky window pane, she could see the red headed woman standing over Doc who was sitting in a chair. The woman straddled him and pulled his face up towards hers. As Sarah stood there watching, a silvery light began to lift from inside of Doc. The woman leaned down to kiss him. As her lips met his, the light went into her. His body grew pale and limp as she pulled away from him. Doc fell with a sickening thud to the floor.

Backing away from the window as quickly as she could, Sarah stumbled over an old milk pale that had been left by the porch. The clattering brought Sarah to her senses. She saw Maggie tied up on a post. Her fingers fought to undo the knot and hang on to Gabe at the same time. As Sarah swung herself up into the saddle, the woman came outside. For a split second, Sarah could have sworn that her eyes were as black as coal, but then they switched to an ordinary shade of green. Sarah dug her heels into Maggie's flanks. The old horse wasn't used to being treated so roughly, and she broke out in a startled run.

"No!" The woman screeched at the top of her lungs as Sarah rode away.

Sarah's only thought was that she had to get away. She couldn't let that woman have Gabriel. Maggie's steps were becoming uneven as she ran, but Sarah urged her forward. She glanced behind her. In the distance, she could see a dark horse in pursuit. The rider's red hair flamed in the sunset's light. By some instinct, Sarah felt driven to the Kiowa's tribe. She held Gabriel in one hand and the reins in the other, praying that Maggie wouldn't give up just yet.

As the teepees came into view, Sarah looked behind her once more. The other rider was gaining on them. Maggie was struggling now. Sarah rode into the middle of the camp and slid off of her borrowed horse. Pale Sparrow rushed out of her teepee to see what the commotion was about. The braves were gathered in a circle around a fire. Their faces were painted, and they danced wildly around the flames. Sarah hid behind Pale Sparrow as the red haired woman stopped her horse on the edge of the camp.

"The child is mine!" The woman's voice rang out over the camp. "He is owed to me." She stepped brazenly towards Sarah. Her voice seemed melodic, almost mesmerizing.

At the sound of her voice, Wandering Coyote emerged from his dwelling. He was chanting and carrying tobacco leaves. He made his way to the fire the braves were dancing around, and he cast the leaves into the flames. As the smell filled the air, the red haired woman backed away as if the scent was casting her back. She looked dazed as she blinked through the smoke. A few braves that had not been dancing circled around behind the woman and cried out as they caught her by the wrists and ankles. She tried to kick free, but they held her fast. Her eyes morphed back into black, soulless pits as her anger swelled.

Two of the men by her feet pulled off her shoes. Sarah gasped. Beneath the shoes, the woman's feet were cloven hooves. She kicked with more vigor, trying to break free from their grasp.

Wandering Coyote spoke in his native tongue, and Pale Sparrow translated for Sarah as he spoke, "You have been seen. Deer Woman, you have no more power of these people. Your face is known. Your spell is broken. You are cast out."

The woman screamed in agony as the braves released her. She mounted her black stallion and stormed off into the darkness. Soon not even her hair was visible on the horizon. Sarah had stood in shock through the entire process. She clutched Gabriel so tightly that her fingers were turning white.

"What just happened?" She was shaking as she faced Pale Sparrow.

"That was a Deer Woman. They feed on the souls of men. In your stories she would be called a Succubus. Wandering Coyote saw her in a vision. He knew she would come. Tobacco smoke drives them away, but the only way to send one away for good is to look at her cloven feet. In the old stories past down, it is said that the Deer Woman will mate with a man and have his baby. Once the child is born, she must sacrifice it to maintain her youth. If she is unable to do so, or if her identity is revealed before she can complete the sacrifice, she will become mortal."

"What about the baby?" Sarah looked down at Gabriel, "Will he become like her?"

"Our stories only ever speak of Deer Women. We do not have any tales about Deer Men." Pale Sparrow rested her hand on Gabriel's head with a smile.

Sarah breathed a small sigh of relief. She was still trembling. Wandering Coyote walked over and took one of Sarah's hands in his. He brought her and the baby near the fire as the smoke billowed up. He chanted and wafted the smoke over her and Gabriel as he sang. After a few moments a young boy brought Maggie over to her. Sarah nodded in gratitude.

"He has put a blessing around you and the baby." Pale Sparrow gestured to a few braves who had mounted their own horses, "They will accompany you to your village to make sure you make it back safe."

"Thank you." A tear of gratefulness fell down Sarah's cheek as she climbed back on Maggie and rode towards Fort Marshall.

The Kiowa hung back as the town came into view. Sarah finished the ride to her home alone. Jacob was waiting on the porch for her. He ran to greet her. As he held her in his arms, he said, "I was worried sick about you. What happened?"

Sarah recounted what she had seen at Doc's and what had happened with the tribe. Jacob said that he had seen the woman ride out of town and had found Doc dead in his own home. There were no signs of struggle or foul play. It looked as if he had died from natural causes. That night, Sarah and Jacob both stayed awake. The events of the night kept them from their dreams.

The next day, Jacob held the funeral service for Doc. Everyone turned up to reminisce about his loving and helpful nature. Only Sarah and Jacob knew the truth about how he had died. They didn't want to sully his memory with what had really happened. As they bowed their heads to pray a parting prayer over his grave, one of the little girls in the town locked eyes with Gabriel, and for a split second, she thought she saw them go completely black.

COLD ANGEL

OLIVIA BRAUN

The world felt as if it was closing in on the car as Daniel steered them through icy forest roads. Rachel watched as the light snow and fog got thicker and thicker as they ascended. She wasn't worried. She didn't worry about much anymore. And she didn't miss the view. Her body was on its way to her parents' lakeside cabin on December twentieth - very much against their advice - but her mind was trapped six months in the past, in her home in the small town of Lovelock, Nevada, as it had been ever since her daughter was found face-down and motionless in the bathtub.

"This is a good idea," Daniel said. He wiped dirt off the inside of his glasses with his finger, trying to keep his eyes on the road which was lined either side with enormous, snow-blanketed fir trees. "We've got more than enough supplies to last us a month if we get stuck up here."

It was a terrible idea, Rachel thought. But she let him think that he was helping. She didn't care where she was, truthfully, and was under no illusions that the untimely death of her five-year-old daughter would upset her less after a change of scenery. At least it would save them a little money on rent, she thought. Since Kayleigh died, they hadn't been able to sleep in their house. Money was tight before, but even with a loan from her parents, they were about to hit real trouble.

"There's something up ahead," Daniel said. "This is it, right?"

Rachel sat up a little and squinted. She could make out the shape of it through the fog. It was a two-storey cabin with shutters over the small windows, an old swing-chair hanging on the porch and a wooden deer sculpture out front. The roof was covered with a thick layer of snow and the wooden deer was up to his knees in it. It was only three in the afternoon, but between the snow storm and the fog, it was already getting dark. The car's headlights struggled to pick out the cabin through the snow as they got nearer. The cabin took on more features and color as they drove into the fog. The car, a Toyota four-by-four, pushed through the snow and came to a stop with its lights shining through the windows of the cabin. Rachel hadn't seen the place since she was a teenager.

"It hasn't changed a bit," she said, feeling almost disappointed. "I thought it would look different now, but it's exactly how I remember it."

Daniel left the engine running so they could enjoy the heaters for a few precious minutes before heading outside. Rachel sat and let her mind wander to when she was fifteen, without a care in the world, chasing her sister around the forest with a water gun. Rachel missed her sister terribly. She didn't really miss the person her sister had become, the high-flying attorney who had packed up her husband and three kids for Australia five years ago. She missed the girl she had shared her childhood with, rather than the adult who poked her here and there with phone calls from the other side of the world. Rachel missed the girl that she once was, too, and the world she once lived in.

Rachel started a little when Daniel took her hand.

"It can be like it was," he said. "You just need some time away. You've been doing too much. You need to relax."

Rachel said nothing.

She wasn't convinced.

The cabin looked the same, but inside it was emptier, darker.

Just like me, Rachel thought.

*

Rachel kneeled over the fire and prodded it to get it going, her icy breath floating in front of her face, as Daniel was out back gassing up the generator. The fire was slowly coming alive and filling the musty room with a warm, unsteady glow and Rachel looked around. The bare floorboards were freezing under her knees and the floor, as with everything from what she could make out, was covered with a light coating of dust. The lounge was spacious and furnished with floral-patterned furniture that would have been considered luxurious in the eighties. Rachel had considered it luxurious in the eighties. The bookshelf, her father's favorite hideaway on their summer vacations, was still stocked with reserve copies of everything he had at home. There were psychology reference books, reports and a smattering of fiction - DeLillo and Ballard, mostly - which, as a child, she'd found incomprehensible. In the bottom corner of the bookshelf was a small pile of C.S. Lewis and J.R.R. Tolkien he had bought for Rachel and her sister to keep them quiet, to lessen the more destructive or noisy games that disturbed his reading.

Something moved in the top corner of the room, beyond the bookshelf. Rachel stood and grabbed a duster from the box on the floor. It was a cobweb, dangling from side to side. Wiping it away, she hoped that didn't mean spiders. It had been cold enough up here now that they should've all died out, she told herself.

French doors at the back of the room, past a small dining table, looked out onto a long stretch of snow with a small, now-bare apple tree protruding from it, like a black, skeletal hand reaching up from the earth itself. Rachel tried not to look at it. The tree had always unnerved her as a child. She could hear it rustling in the night as she lay awake in her bed trying to pretend she was safe and sound in Nevada. Past the tree was only a wall of shifting whiteness. The fog and the snow obscured completely Jackson Lake which lay beyond.

Rachel stood and watched the ebb and tide of the whiteness which surrounded the cabin and created for her and Daniel a physical barrier between them and the rest of the world. She was grateful for it - and she was sure her parents were grateful for it, having of late become visibly impatient with her relentless grief - but it also filled her with something approaching dread. She had spent the last six months in an unending fit of despair, one which she wasn't sure she would ever see the other side of. There had been nights when she had convinced herself that her life was over, that it was only a matter of moments before she found the courage to take her own life. But she was still here. She was functioning.

She wasn't entertaining those kinds of thoughts anymore. Entering this void of whiteness, a hole in the weather in which she and Daniel could bury themselves, it felt like hiding. It felt like they were tunneling a safe-house for themselves, deep and far from the rest of the world. Rachel was scared that it would take a considerable effort to pull herself out of this tunnel, and worried that she wouldn't have the strength or the will to do it. They had taken themselves out of the world, essentially, and she didn't know if she would want to go back.

The front door slammed shut and startled her out of her gloomy daydream. She took a breath and rubbed the back of her neck.

"Did you get it going?" she said. "The lights are still off."

She turned and peered into the darkness of the hallway through the open lounge door.

"Dan?" she said.

She heard him kicking the wall to knock the snow off his shoes, but it was too dark to see him with only the small fire to light the place. She walked over to the door.

"Did you find my dad's gas store?" she said. "He said there should be enough there to keep us in as much electricity as we can eat for a few months if it comes to it."

She heard him walked up the stairs, but he didn't speak. Frowning, Rachel walked into the dark hallway.

"Dan?" she said, looking up the stairs. "Where are you going?"

She saw a shadow turn the corner at the top of the stairs as she peered up from the bottom.

"You're not going to help me with these freakin' boxes?"

The silence made her uneasy.

What the hell is his problem? she thought.

"Daniel," she called up. "What are you doing?"

There was no response. She held onto the railing, thinking about following him up into the dark upper floor. Something about him being in the dark up there in silence made her stomach turn. He had been distraught about Kayleigh's death, too, but he had recovered. He had been strong for Rachel. His grief was the quiet kind, the detached kind, not like Rachel's, wailing, dribbling and hitting herself periodically for months on end. Rachel's grief was ugly, she knew that. But never for a moment had Daniel been anything less than her own personal therapist and cheerleader. She couldn't ask any more of him. His silence now was getting to her.

"Daniel," she called up again.

She took a few deep breaths and took the first step up the stairs.

Something screeched outside and the cabin was suddenly filled with harsh, white light. Rachel covered her eyes and curled up. Her heart dropped in her chest and she was overcome with panic.

She heard the front door slam behind her and she turned quickly around.

Daniel was stood in the doorway with a grin on his face.

"I got it..." he started, but the panic on Rachel's face stopped him in his tracks. "What's wrong, Rach?" he said.

Rachel looked up the stairs. The upper floor looked empty. She didn't speak for a moment, listening for movement.

"What is it?" Daniel said. He kicked the snow off his shoes and moved to embrace Rachel.

Rachel put up a hand and said, "Were you just in here?"

Daniel looked confused. "What? No," he said. "I was getting the generator going." He pointed to the working lights and said, "See?"

"I thought I heard you come in," Rachel said.

She looked up the stairs. Daniel's face hardened. He looked up the stairs, too.

"Stay here," he said.

"Wait," Rachel said, reaching out after him as he walked quickly up the stairs, his boots knocking hard on the wooden slats.

He reached the top of the stairs and looked around. Rachel waited with bated breath. He walked away from the top of the stairs and

Rachel listened to his boots on the floorboards. She heard him opening doors, entering rooms, walking around. Rachel put her hand through her hair and tried to calm herself. She leaned against the wall. Something cold and wet made her move her hand away. It was water. She looked at the wall and saw in a faint outline, half destroyed by her touching it, the wet outline of a small hand on the yellow-beige floral wallpaper.

She took a step back and brought her hand to her mouth. Tears hit her eyes and her lungs locked down and stopped her breath.

It was a child's hand-print, still wet.

It was still dripping down the wall, and after a few seconds, it had become a shapeless, watery mark.

The sound of Daniel's footsteps grew louder and he appeared at the top of the stairs.

"There's no-one up here," he said, walking back down. "You sure you heard something?"

Rachel looked at him with tears in her eyes. She swallowed hard and glanced at him to the now-unrecognizable wet spot on the wall.

"What's wrong?" he said, embracing her.

She let herself get lost in his arms and closed her eyes. She started to breathe again.

You're being a freakin' idiot, she told herself. You've lost it. Get yourself together, woman.

"What is it?" he said. "Is it this place? I know it's a little spooky in the dark with the storm and all, but we'll make it cozy, you'll see." He moved back and took her face in his cold hands and looked at her with concern. "Are you OK?" he said.

Rachel dried her eyes and nodded. She attempted a smile. "I just got a little spooked, I guess," she said. "I'm sorry. I'm being childish."

Daniel hugged her close.

"I love you," Rachel said.

"More than anything," Daniel replied, as was their routine.

*

The first night was passing slowly. Rachel and Daniel lay in bed facing in opposite directions, not touching, not speaking, waiting to fall asleep, just like they had done every other night in recent memory. When they were awake and walking around in the daylight, Rachel had moments where she felt things were almost as they were before. She could never pretend Kayleigh was just in the next room - the constant and intense longing in her gut would never go away - but things between her and Daniel at times could be described as normal. He could be charming and loving and kind. He couldn't be funny again yet, even though he'd started trying recently. But when the sun went down and they lay in bed together with nothing but their thoughts, Rachel could hardly bring herself to say his name or look him in the eye. Maybe he felt the same way.

But I wasn't the one who let her drown, Rachel thought.

She closed the thought down almost as soon as she had it. It wasn't healthy, she knew that. It wasn't anyone's fault, that's what she kept telling herself. But, deep down, there was a dark place inside her reserved for such thoughts.

It had been Daniel's turn to give Kayleigh a bath. Rachel could hear her laughing and playing for a while. He was telling her a story about a friendly monster. Rachel fell asleep with a book in her hands. When it dropped from her grasp and hit the floor, it woke her up. There was no laughter to be heard, then. The silence made her feel sick to her stomach, before she'd even known what had happened. When she walked into the bathroom, Kayleigh was face-down in the water. She'd slipped and bumped her head, that's what they said. She was unconscious as the water filled her little lungs. Rachel didn't know what happened after that. She has flashes of memory here and there, of blue lips and cold hands, but nothing substantial to hold onto. She didn't know where Daniel was. She didn't know what she did. She woke up in the hospital. Daniel said he had just stepped away for two minutes, that she was safe when he left her.

But she wasn't safe.

If she was safe, Rachel thought, she wouldn't have drowned.

Rachel lay on her side in bed. The moon was reflecting off the snow outside and it gave the room a light glow. Rachel's eyes were wide open. She was tired, but she couldn't sleep. All she could do, as on any other night, was lay there and think, if she was safe then she wouldn't have drowned.

Rachel slipped the covers off her and wrapped a bathrobe around her on top of her pajamas. She kicked on her slippers and walked downstairs in search of a hot drink.

The light in the kitchen blinded Rachel when she flipped it on. She covered her eyes and stood still for a moment to let her tired eyes adjust. She started making herself a cup of cocoa and she studied her reflection in the night-blackened windows. She had bags under her eyes and her long, auburn hair was a tangled mess. She looked at herself long enough to realize that she couldn't see anything on the outside. The windows were open to the outside world but acted only as dark mirrors for those inside. The thought made Rachel's blood run cold.

Rachel's feet ran cold too. Turning, she saw that the back door had come open slightly and was drifting ever more open with the breeze. The snow storm had calmed, thankfully, but it was still freezing outside. Rachel pushed the door closed gently so as to not wake Daniel. She looked at the cuckoo clock on the wall. It was three in the morning. Rachel stirred her cocoa and took the kettle off the stove. When she flipped off the light switch, she saw a straight line of moonlight coming from behind her.

The back door was ajar again.

Nothing to worry about, Rachel said. I just didn't close it tightly, that's all. That's all it is.

Rachel placed her cocoa down on the kitchen table and walked across the tiled floor to the back door, her slippers scraping as she dragged her feet. Touching the handle of the door, she looked out. Now that it was dark inside, she could see outside.

There was nothing there, just snow and moonlight and the big black hand that was the dead apple tree.

Rachel pushed the door closed gently until it clicked. She took the key from off a hook on the wall to lock it shut. She pressed the key into the lock, but it was stiff. Jangling it, it still wouldn't go.

"Come on," Rachel whispered.

She crouched down and looked inside the keyhole. It was dark. There didn't seem to be anything blocking the way. She took the large key and guided it in with both hands, making completely sure not to twitch or tremble. She didn't want it to go off course. Once the key was in firmly, completely, she turned it slowly and with a small clunk it was locked.

"That wasn't so hard, was it?" she said to herself.

Standing up, she saw a small, pale face peering up from the bottom of the back door window.

Rachel recoiled and fell onto her back, knocking the wind out of herself.

She looked up at the back door window and the face peered over the bottom frame at her with large black eyes. Rachel tried to scream, but her breath hadn't come back. She fumbled around behind her for the light switch. The back door handle was being turned from outside, rattled.

Rachel spun around, flipped the kitchen light on and turned back to the door.

The face was gone.

Rachel caught her breath and didn't blink.

In the light, she could see now the window pane had misted up under where the face had been, under where its breath had come into contact with the glass. Something was written in the condensation, a word smudged into the moisture with a small finger.

Rachel took a tentative step forward to read what it said.

It said: D A D D Y

*

By the time her screaming had woken Daniel and he'd gotten downstairs, the word had faded on the glass.

"I saw someone," Rachel said, pointing from where she sat on the floor with her knees tucked up to her chest. "It was a little kid, I think. There at the back door. Looking in."

Daniel kneeled on the floor beside her and held her. "There's no-one out here, honey," he said. "We're in the middle of nowhere. There's no one else for miles around. It's OK, hush now."

"I saw it," she said.

Daniel kissed her on the forehead and looked her in the eyes as if searching for the truth in there.

"I saw it," she repeated.

Daniel and Rachel didn't sleep for the rest of the night. Daniel stayed up until dawn with her. Neither spoke, but rather sat and read on opposite sides of the room. Daniel was comforting when he spoke, but the fact that he rarely spoke belied his real feelings. He looked almost angry, Rachel thought. There was a tension there, just under the surface. He smiled a little too easily, spoke a little too calmly. Dawn came at long last and with it, Rachel and Daniel prepared breakfast and planned their day. In the light of day, Rachel's fears about the place died away. She walked out to the lake through the back door and didn't give the dead apple tree a second glance. She didn't look for strangers or jump at animal sounds. She simply walked to the lake to see if it had changed.

Jackson Lake sat in the shadow of the magnificent Teton mountains. In the icy weather, they looked like death incarnate, promising only starvation and frost-bite and a painful end in grand isolation. The lake was sealed with a thin sheet of ice which twinkled in the sunlight and the surrounding forests were white with their trees bent and misshapen from the weight of the snow.

Rachel dug in the snow for a moment and dug up a large stone. Walking to the edge of the lake, she threw the stone and listened to it crack through the ice further in and splash as it sank into the depths of the lake.

She stood for a moment and enjoyed the silence. She took a baby step forward and let the water that was coming out from under the cracked ice at the edge touch the bottom of her boots. The cold was creeping through her wool gloves and she started to feel a slow pain coming on, the raw stinging of the water from the snow seeping onto her skin. Rachel thought about how it would feel if that was all over her body, how bad the pain would be and how long it would last if she threw herself into the lake.

The wind rushed through the nearby trees and Rachel closed her eyes and listened to the sound of the branches scraping up against one another. In the noise, she thought she heard words, faint, masked by the wind, or perhaps made from it.

"Dee-add," came the whisper. "Deeeeee-add."

Rachel closed her eyes tighter and listened hard. It was like someone was whispering on the wind, only not quite. It didn't sound like a person.

"Deeee-ad," it came clear as day.

Rachel opened her eyes. She heard it.

"Daddy," it whispered.

Suddenly, a hand touched her back. Rachel leaped around and swore.

"Daniel!" she said.

"Christ," he said. "I'm sorry. I called you. I thought you knew I was here."

He put his arms around her waist from behind and she faced the lake. She was tense. She looked around to see if anyone else was lurking.

I must be going crazy, she thought.

"What are you doing out here anyway?" he said.

"I was just looking," Rachel said, trying not to sound too scared.

"It's a beautiful place," Daniel said. "It could use a little sunshine, but it's real nice up here, don't you think?"

Daniel was holding her tight. A little too tight, Rachel thought.

"I could live up here, I think," Daniel said. "No crowds, no traffic, no noise, just us and mother nature."

Rachel turned in his arms and faced him. She tried to smile.

"You're right," Daniel said. "No internet. We'd hate it."

Daniel smiled, but there was something behind the smile. Rachel didn't know what it was. She'd never seen it before. It unnerved her. It was, again, as if his smile was too genuine, too easy. She used to be able to read him like an open book. Lately, for the past year or so, he'd constructed a wall. Rachel had no idea what went on in his head.

"We better head inside," Rachel said. "Looks like that storm's coming back."

Daniel didn't move. He just looked at her, thinking.

"Daniel?" she said.

He nodded and snapped out of whatever it was that had hold of his attention. "Let's go in," he said. "You're right. Let's batten down the hatches and make that fire earn its keep." He laughed as he took her hand and they walked away from the shore of the lake. His laugh unsettled Rachel, but she didn't know why.

*

Rachel waited impatiently for the night to come. She and Daniel sat by the fire and read, talking very little. She read her dog-eared C.S. Lewis while he poured over her father's textbooks. She wanted to be rid of Daniel and his odd stares and long silences. She wanted to go back out to the lake. Whatever it is, she thought, it's out there. And it's trying to talk to me.

Craziness be damned, she thought. If I'm crazy, I'm crazy, but I have to see.

There was a small part of her that hoped beyond all hope that maybe, just maybe, it was Kayleigh. Rachel had never put much faith in the supernatural or religion, but she had always held out a little bit of hope that there was something else, after all this. Now, having lost the light of her life, she had more hope than ever.

But why would Kayleigh come to her now, after all this time? And why here?

"I think I'm going to head up to bed," Daniel said, yawning and snapping his book closed. "Are you coming?"

Rachel tried to look calm. She smiled as warmly as she could manage. "I'm gonna stay up for a bit longer," she said. "I want to read some more."

"Trapped in Narnia," Daniel said as he kissed her on the top of her head. "Don't stay up too long, hey? I'm just upstairs if you need anything."

"OK," Rachel said.

The next wait was the longest of all. Rachel timed herself. She would wait two hours before going outside. Daniel was sure to be asleep by then. She tried to distract herself with the book, but while her eyes did move over the words none of them entered her mind. Her thoughts were racing. She felt nauseous with worry about herself, about her mental health.

This is how it starts, she thought. It seems a little weird, but you accept it. Then it gets weirder and weirder and you accept it easier and easier until one day you're dressed all in white and lining up for pills in your ward in the nut house.

The clock in the lounge was a smiling Felix the cat. His whiskers were the hands. Rachel had begged her dad to buy that clock one summer when she was a girl. It had taken three whole days to persuade him, and just as long again to persuade him to put it up in the lounge. Rachel stared at Felix until his face was burned onto the back of her eyeballs. His whiskers moved painfully slowly, tick tick ticking along.

Rachel must have dozed off, because after a long blink, it was time. It was three in the morning. Daniel had been upstairs for four hours. There's no way he's awake, Rachel thought.

She pulled on her big winter coat with the fur hood, slipped into her boots, and walked into the kitchen. She turned off the kitchen light before she moved to the back door. It looked lonely outside. It was only in the dark that the isolation of the place really hit Rachel. They were hundreds and hundreds of miles from anyone. Daniel said he hoped she could rest easier, but, if anything, it was making things worse.

Here I am, she thought, walking out into a snow storm at three in the morning looking for ghosts. I have absolutely cracked up.

She opened the door slowly and silently. The snow had piled up a little at the door, the wind having blown it against the house. Rachel looked around with her icy breath hanging in front of her face. She looked beyond the black hand of the apple tree, to the forest beyond, and she squinted to try to see through the light but constant and swirling snowfall to Jackson Lake, but she couldn't. Rachel stepped outside and closed the door, listening for the click of the catch.

The moon was full and bright and the snow-covered ground glowed in its rays. Dark spots in the snow caught Rachel's eye. There were two of them, right in front of her. Rachel covered her eyes with her gloved hands and looked down.

Her heart almost stopped.

Footprints.

It was a pair of child's footprints.

No bigger or smaller than Kayleigh's were, Rachel thought.

She took a deep breath and took a step forward in the direction of the lake, where the footprints were pointing. And as she stepped another set of footprints appeared in front of her. She kept walking, and step after step revealed child's footsteps in front of her. She was being led.

Looking up, peering through the snow, Rachel caught a glimpse of a child running away, its arms flapping by its sides as it ran as fast as it could. It looked back over its shoulder.

It was Kayleigh.

Rachel stopped and dropped to her knees. She was overcome with joy, just seeing her daughter's face.

Kayleigh looked scared.

"Daddy!" Rachel heard her call.

Rachel stood and ran as fast as she could through the snow. The storm was beginning to calm and the half-frozen lake appeared in front of her out of the fog. Kayleigh was gone, but her footprints led to the water. Rachel looked around, panicked.

"Kayleigh," she said. "Kayleigh, please."

"Daddy," a whisper came behind her.

Rachel spun around and was facing the cabin. No-one was stood behind her, but as the storm subsided and the fog drifted away, Rachel could see the cabin clearly. In the bedroom window, Daniel stood watching her.

"Daniel?" Rachel said.

He was fully dressed in his coat, hat, and gloves. He was completely motionless, utterly expressionless. His eyes were locked on Rachel. In the glow of the moon, his face was totally white, and his eyes were deep in shadow. He stared down at Rachel with something that looked like contempt. She had never seen any expression even resembling it on his face before.

He looked like he hated her.

He's been waiting up this whole time, Rachel suddenly thought. But why?

"Daddy," came the voice behind her.

Rachel turned and suddenly, there was Kayleigh, stood with her feet in the icy water of the lake.

"Daddy," she said.

"Baby," Rachel said. She reached out to touch her but stopped just short from fear of making her leave.

"Daddy," she said again.

Rachel started to lose all feeling in her body, starting with her hands. They tingled and then went dead. A feeling of horror swept over her as she started to lose all control of herself as if possessed. Her hands moved forwards of their own accord.

"Wait," Rachel said. "No."

Her hands grabbed hold of Kayleigh, holding her by her shoulders. Rachel fought it with every fiber of her being, but she wasn't in control.

"Daddy," Kayleigh said, "what are you doing?"

Rachel heard her own voice say, "Hush, baby. This won't hurt."

Rachel pushed Kayleigh down in the water. She didn't fight. She smiled, thinking they were playing a game.

"Daddy," she said again, "what-"

Her head was pushed under the water. She barely struggled. Rachel's hands held her there. Kayleigh hardly moved. She trusted it was a game, right until the moment before she passed out when there was a small flash of panic and a muffled scream. And then she was drowned.

"No," Rachel said. "No, no, no."

Her hands wouldn't move. They held Kayleigh's lifeless body down in the icy water.

"Let me go!" she screamed, and suddenly her hands were released.

Rachel fell backward into the snow, screaming and crying. It was him, she thought. He did it on purpose! He drowned her! He drowned her with his own hands! That's what she wanted to show me!

"Rachel," the voice came from behind her.

She turned and stood. He offered his hand, but she didn't take it.

"What are you doing out here?" he said.

Rachel sniffed back her tears.

"I, uh, couldn't sleep," he said. "And I saw you thrashing around out here. You're worrying me, honey."

Rachel couldn't find the words to speak.

"You're worrying everyone," he said. "They don't know what you might do to yourself."

That was it, she thought. That was why now, why here. He'd brought her out here to kill her, to make it look like she'd finally had enough and taken her own life. It was a warning. "Daddy," she said. She was warning her.

"Rachel," he said, "I'm talking to you."

"Stay away from me," she whispered. "I know what you are."

Confused, he nearly laughed. "Rachel, I don't know what you mean. What am I?"

"I know what you did," she said.

His half-smile dropped. He became serious. "What did I do?" he said.

Rachel took a step back and looked behind her. She was on the edge of the lake, her boots in the water.

"It's so quiet up here, isn't it?" he said, taking a step towards her. "You could get away with anything up here."

"Why did you do it?" Rachel said, bursting into tears. Then, screaming, she said, "You drowned her! Why?!"

"I don't know!" he shouted back, leaning towards her. "You don't have reasons for things like this!"

Rachel looked at him, stunned.

"I was going to kill us all," he said, quieter. "I can't take this world anymore. I was going to kill us all, so we could be together. We could finally be as happy as we deserve to be."

Rachel broke down in tears and said, "Kayleigh was happy!"

Daniel wiped tears away from his own eyes and stepped towards Rachel.

"Stay away!" she screamed.

Daniel grabbed her arm with one hand and with the other took out a hunting knife from a sheath under his coat. "Nobody will understand," he said. "Nobody really cares anyway. We're better off this way."

"No!" Rachel screamed. "You're fucking insane!"

She punched and kicked at Daniel, splashing in the water, but he held her still and brought the knife against her chest, the point over her heart. "Hush, baby," he said. "This won't hurt."

A small voice came from behind Daniel. "Daddy," it said.

Daniel turned, and in that moment Rachel grabbed his knife, twisted it back and plunged it deep into his stomach. He screamed for his life and fell to his knees. Rachel stepped away, leaving the knife inside him, as he dropped onto his hands and knees in the water, turning back towards the cabin. In front of him stood Kayleigh. The icy water turned red around him as he looked at his dead daughter in utter terror.

Rachel moved to the shore and watched as he shook his head. "No," he said. He looked at Rachel and said, "Come with me. Be with us." Blood spilled out of his mouth and he collapsed face down in the water.

"You're going to a different place," Rachel said.

Daniel's body went limp in the water. Rachel heard his dying breath, a long final exhalation. And he was gone.

"Mummy," a voice came, and with that Kayleigh vanished into a flurry of snow carried on the wind.

The storm was coming back. The clouds were drawing in overhead, shutting out the moonlight. The world was getting darker, but Rachel felt herself straightening up, the fog of grief lifting from her mind.

She trudged back through the snow as it got heavier and heavier. Slamming the back door behind her, she felt entirely closed off from everyone. The cabin was consumed by the storm. Rachel sat on the kitchen floor with her back to the wall. And though she started to cry, she was filled with this unshakable feeling the likes of which she hadn't felt for years, not since the day Kayleigh was born. Rachel felt that even if the storm worsened, she would be able to survive it.

She could survive anything.

The End.

WE ALL FALL DOWN

OLIVIA BRAUN

TAMI BARRERA

Chapter One

In every movie he'd seen, Mark Allen Geer noticed that spooky hospitals and corridors were always darker than they should have been. Why was that? He didn't realize the fact until he entered the halls of Fern Heights Rehabilitation and Assisted Living.

He set his large hands on the wheels of his chair and stopped its motion forward. He looked around and over his shoulder when the chair jogged forward. An attendant had stumbled into him when he'd abruptly stopped.

"Sorry, sir. I didn't mean to run into you."

Mark ran his eyes up the blue scrubs to the sheepish face of the young attendant. His mood told him to scowl fiercely and cuss the young man out. But for once, he didn't. He clenched his jaw, nodded and turned back around.

"Why is it so dark in here?" He asked loudly. "Where's the lights? Why does it have to be so dark?"

"This is only temporary, sir." The attendant, whose name was Josh, said in a respectful voice. Mark tried not to like him. He'd been forced to come to this rehab. He'd just returned from his third tour in Iraq, each one extended to the maximum amount of time allowed. He considered himself young. He would be turning 30 in a few months. His plan had always been to retire from the military and live in a small house somewhere yelling at kids to get off the lawn.

It had only come to an end because he'd been shot. It made him mad. It made him furious, to be completely honest. He had no family, having lost both his parents as a small child and raised by grandparents who were involved in a fatal car accident when he was about to graduate from high school.

He'd always been interested in the military. When his life took such a violent turn, he took advantage of the events and signed up for the Army. He wanted to be on the front lines. He wanted to be where all the action was, killing the enemy with precision.

He'd been doing just what he wanted, just what he loved to do, when the bullet from a hidden sniper up on the roof of a nearby building had entered his spine, severing it so precisely, there was no way to restore the use of his legs. He would never walk again. That put an end to his career in the military. He wasn't educated enough to have a job behind a desk. His body had been left a wreck after the shooting. His life changed forever.

He'd been an angry young man before entering the military. Now that his passion was ripped from his hands in the prime of his life, all he wanted to do was die.

That was what he'd told the hospital psychiatrist during their last session. Quickly after that, they'd shipped him here, where the government could keep a proper eye on him. They didn't want him to turn into another statistic. Just another returning injured veteran offing himself, handing over the ultimate sacrifice for his country.

He was proud of his country and did, in fact, fight to protect it. If he killed himself, it wouldn't be because he was mad about the war. It would be because he was mad he couldn't fight in it anymore.

He realized the attendant had continued speaking and focused in on his words, wondering how much he'd missed while stewing in his bitterness.

"...adjustments. They plan to be done with the remodeling in the next month. Until then, some of the lights are kept on in certain corridors because they are in the process of replacing the lamps."

Mark was satisfied he hadn't missed much. He stared down the corridor to the left and then to the right. This Victorian style home was massive. It had once been a prosperous plantation house. Now it served as the rehabilitation clinic for injured soldiers.

He moved through the foyer, easily wheeling around the reception desk, following Josh and the other attendant, a huge black man called Steven Long. Mark thought of a bouncer as soon as he saw the man.

But this wasn't a bar, there would be no alcohol and the nurses weren't as pretty as barmaids would be. And he didn't have to tip them.

"This is your room, Mr. Geer. It has been fitted with the equipment you'll need to make your stay more comfortable."

"I'm not going to get better," Mark grumbled without looking at either attendant. "So I think my stay is gonna be pretty long."

Josh just nodded, opening the door, going in and holding it open wide so Mark could get through. He looked around the room, slightly distracted by the thought that he could feel a headache coming on and for some odd reason, his legs felt cold. He wasn't usually able to feel his legs at all. So the fact that they were cold made him confused.

"Okay, thanks. Thanks. This will be fine. I appreciate it. Okay." He made a wide circle with his chair and nodded as Steven and Josh brought in his trunk and two duffle bags. He eyed the small pile and sighed, realizing everything he owned in the world was packed in those three items.

Josh and Steven went back out the door. Josh turned back. "We'll be serving lunch in a half hour, sir. That should be enough time for you to get somewhat settled. If you would like to have lunch in here, that would suitable. Or would you care to go to the dining hall?"

"I'll go to the dining hall." Mark wanted to check out the other patients and the staff on duty. He'd never been to this rehab before. He'd never been shot before so there hadn't been a need for one. He wasn't going to isolate himself in this creepy room all the time. He needed to get out and explore. But first, he would look for possible enemies and cohorts. He would assess the situation and act accordingly, just like his favorite drill sergeant, Col. Drew Baxter-Hall, who yelled at him all the way through boot camp so long ago, had advised him to do on every mission he went on.

Chapter Two

He closed the door behind the two attendants and pushed the wheels on his chair so that he rolled backwards slightly. He stared at the room around him. It had been modernized but the wallpaper gave away its age. The entire building was built in 1923 and totally remodeled twice, once in 1976 and once in 2006. Mark was slightly annoyed that in the second remodeling, they hadn't bothered to put up new wallpaper. Or paneling. Anything would have been better than the same old wallpaper from the seventies. A strange greenish brown color. Not even anything cheerful. At the very least, colors that didn't remind him of the dusty plains in Iraq. Brown. Brown everywhere. All shades of it.

He shook his head and wheeled over to the edge of the bed. He pushed himself out of the chair and onto the bed, using the motion of the bouncing bed to pull his legs up and stretch them out in front of him. The bed groaned a little. It was unnerving. There was no reason for it to make any sounds. He was a big man but not *that* big. He weighed a steady 185 at his most muscular, standing 5'11".

He looked down at the bed. The sound of groaning continued but was faded...muffled...

His heart pounded harder. Was the sound coming from under the bed? He felt stupid. There were no monsters under the bed.

"You're not going stir-crazy, Mark. It's not going to happen. There's no monsters under the bed. There's no danger in this room. That's why you're here. Remember? So you can't do yourself any harm."

He kept mumbling comforting words as his heart hammered in his chest and he leaned over slowly to look at the floor beside the bed. He wouldn't see anything, he knew that. He wouldn't be able to lean over far enough to actually see under the bed anyway.

He felt like a fool, staring down at the thin yellow carpet. He was a grown man. Why was he so nervous? He sat back up straight, frustrated with himself. Now he didn't want to be on the bed. He wanted to be back in his chair. He wanted to go sit by the window and stare out at the landscape around the big house-turned-hospital. He wondered if his window faced the nearby woods or the parking lot.

With his luck, it would be the parking lot.

He scooted his body over and moved his legs so they were hanging off the edge of the bed, ignoring the fear that shot through him, picturing hands coming out from under the bed, grabbing his ankles and dragging him under. He yanked on the chair to drag it close again and pushed himself back from the bed to the chair.

Once he was settled in, he rolled to the window, blinking a few times at the bright light coming in from outside. His eyes adjusted to it quickly. He stared out with a blank expression, taking in as far into the distance as he could. He could only see a few people moving about on the lawn. It turned out he could see half of the yard and half of the parking lot. Beyond that he could see part of the street and the distance was lined with woods and mountains. That suited him fine. He was determined to try to find good things to focus on. There had to be something that would make this place a little less like Hell than it already appeared to be. He stared at the horizon, wishing he was a bird that could take flight and get out of this torment he was in.

He looked away from the window. The room was situated so that anything he needed was at waist level, his faucet, a small fridge set in the corner, the dresser was long and short, a full length mirror was attached to the back of the door. He was grateful to see the door to the bathroom slightly ajar. He was glad to have a bathroom in his room. That meant he didn't have to worry about going out into the common room to get to a community bathroom, like he'd had to at the last facility he was in.

He felt a rush of cold air and sucked in a quick deep breath of surprise. The hairs on his arm and the back of his neck stood on end. He shivered. Frowning, he stared around the room. There was something wrong…something felt *wrong*. He didn't want to be in there anymore. He pushed the chair forward forcefully and opened the door.

Just as he went through the doorway, he noticed a difference in how he felt. The headache that had been threatening him the entire time he was in the room almost immediately vanished. He could no longer feel his legs, cold *or* warm.

He rolled away from the door, glancing over his shoulder as it closed behind him. He narrowed his eyes.

"Mr. Geer, are you all right? Would you like a tour of the facilities while we wait for lunch to be put on the table?" He looked down the short hallway to a woman who was standing just behind the reception desk. She wasn't dressed casually like a receptionist. She was dressed like a nurse.

"Who are you?" he asked, trying not to sound blunt.

"My name is Barbara Prince. You can call me Babs. Everyone else does."

"All right, Babs. Yes," he nodded. "I'd like a tour of the facilities, thanks."

She gave him a smile that made him feel more comfortable than he had in a very long time. It was still too dark and he didn't like that. He didn't like the shadows that were cast by the shade in the hallway and down the corridors. But something in the woman's smile made him feel warm…peaceful. She went around his chair and grasped the handles, leaning forward to look at him. She smelled like strawberries.

Mark liked strawberries.

"I'll push you, Mr. Geer, if you'd like to take a rest from it."

"Yeah, thanks. That's always nice."

"Do you have a cell phone, sir? Most people have one to entertain them."

Mark shook his head. "I don't have a cell phone. Nobody to call."

"You have no relatives? No friends?"

"Nope."

"That sounds very sad, sir. I'm so sorry."

"Maybe I'll make some friends here."

Babs leaned forward and looked at him. "Well, you've made one so far."

Chapter Three

The dining room was huge, compared to the number of current residents in the facility. It was well lit, making Mark feel just a bit safer. As soon as she pushed him through the doors, Babs stopped and came around to the side, kneeling next to him. He looked down at her curiously.

She pointed to a group of people at a large round table near the far end of the room. "Those are your co-residents. They reside in the same hall as you, in the other rooms, you know."

"Okay." He nodded, staring at the group. There were four people at the table, three men and a woman.

"These other two tables are for the other two floors. And those over there are for the other halls on the other side of the facility."

"So do those people at my table, they here for mental problems like me?"

Babs raised her eyebrows. "Is that why you are here, Mark?"

"I thought you people already knew about the patients you bring in here."

Babs smiled, shaking her head. "I am sometimes out of the loop. But I did know that we were receiving a vet on suicide watch. That must be you."

Mark snorted. "Say the wrong thing to the wrong person one time and find yourself shipped off to a prison hospital."

Babs giggled, a strange sound that Mark didn't expect. "This is not a prison, sir, I promise."

"Call me Mark." More than anything, he wanted her to call him Mark. She gave off a warm, inviting presence and he enjoyed just having her near. He was glad she wasn't insulted when he called the place a prison. He vowed silently to be a little friendlier. He tried a smile. He knew it had to look half-hearted but he was grateful to see her laugh again.

"You don't have to worry, Mark. You won't be treated like a prisoner here, I promise."

"Well, okay, if you promise." He said. He felt stupid. He felt like that was the stupidest thing he could have said. He clenched his jaw in frustration. "Well, let's get over there already." He grunted, grasping the wheels and shoving himself forward, practically knocking Babs off balance. She hurried to stand and follow him. His cheeks were burning in embarrassment and regret. He hadn't meant to be so abrupt.

When he reached the table, Babs was by his side once again. "Hello everyone." She said with a huge grin.

"Hello, Babs!" The men lifted their hands. One of them stood up and bowed slightly from the waist.

"Ma'am." He said, winking at her.

"How are you today, Babs?" The woman asked.

"I'm doing really well today, Jenny. I want to introduce you to our newest resident, Sgt. Mark Geer. He is recovering from a spinal injury."

"Iraq?" The man who had stood up asked him as he sat. "Lybia? Afghanistan?"

"Iraq." Mark responded. "You?"

"Lybia. Got my eye shot out and took two more to the chest. Gonna have breathing problems all my life but I'm still here, aren't I? And glad of it."

"Mark, this is Jenny Garcia, Victor Tennant, David Beckett..." The man with one eye nodded in acknowledgement. "and Bob Havers. They are the residents in the rooms that surround yours."

"Thank you, Babs." He nodded up at her. Then he nodded at the group. He noticed that one place set at the table did not have a chair in front of it. He easily wheeled himself up to the table. "Convenient." He said.

"I think it would have been awfully rude if they had not set a place for you, Sgt. Geer." Jenny leaned to him and whispered dramatically, as if she was telling a secret. "They knew you were coming and had a wheelchair."

He nodded at her. "I suppose it would have been rude, Jenny."

"I hope you are comfortable in that room, Sgt. Geer." Bob spoke up. He was missing his right arm. He was short and heavy, something that must have happened after his time in service. Mark was sure he was too fatty to have been in shape to fight in combat anywhere recently. He looked like he could have been a stocky, well-built scrapper at one point but now...he was probably doing all he could to lift a jelly donut to his lips.

"I think I will be." Mark nodded. "Don't know why I wouldn't be."

"Stop being like that, Bob." Jenny slapped the air playfully in Bob's direction. She looked at Mark. "He's being a scoundrel, trying to get you freaked out, is all."

"How's that gonna happen?" Mark looked at each of the group members, confused.

Jenny raised her eyebrows. "Oh, so you don't know about that room?"

Mark closed his eyes for a moment. What did he need to know about that room? "Okay, Jenny, I'll bite. What happened in the room? Someone kill themselves? Kill someone else? Get stuck in the closet for forty years, only to be discovered living on spiders, rats and..."

"Sgt. Geer, Don't be facetious." Jenny responded, seriously. She covered her mouth with her hand and looked around as if afraid they would be heard. "That's where Jerry Wayne Hall lived."

Mark looked from one to another.

"Jenny, now you're going to be the one to put a fright in him."

Mark wasn't sure what they were talking about but if someone said he was going to be frightened one more time, he might blow his top.

To his amazement, Babs spoke up. He hadn't even realized she was still there.

"I don't think anything is going to frighten Sgt. Geer," she said, firmly, drawing the attention of the rest of the group, as well. "He volunteered for extended tours and has seen quite a lot of action."

"But you didn't tell him about that room?" Jenny shook her head. "You should have."

"What's the deal? What's up with the room?" Mark frowned at Jenny, trying to mentally drag the information from the woman. She turned her green eyes to him.

"A bad soldier lived in there."

Chapter Four

Mark was beginning to think Jenny must be simple. Why else would she be acting like a little girl? The thought made him pull back his temper somewhat. He didn't cuss out simpletons.

"What do you mean 'a bad soldier'?" he asked, forcing his voice to be more gentle.

"She means that the last guy that stayed in that room killed a bunch of people, other people that lived here. That was a long time ago, Jen, during the 80's. There's no need to bring it up now. Why would you even tell him that anyway?" Victor was shaking his head. He had a thick accent that signified to Mark he'd been raised in another country. He didn't want to hazard a guess which one but Puerto Rico came to mind right away.

"Some guy killed a bunch of people in my room back in the 80's?" He raised one eyebrow. "Okay. So is his ghost living in there now?"

"Could be." Jenny said, softly.

"Jenny!" Victor shook his head. "What's the matter with you? Just because things like that scare *you* doesn't mean it's gonna scare *him* and why would you want him to be scared anyway?"

"I don't want him to be scared."

Mark looked from one face to another, trying to figure out when he'd time-warped back to high school. He'd lost his appetite and just wanted to get away from these people. They were nuts.

His hands went to the wheels of his chair to push away but he stopped when he felt a soft hand cover one of his. He looked down and followed the arm up to Babs' smiling face.

She shook her head, leaned over and whispered, "Don't give up on them, Mark. Give them a chance. They're good people, I promise."

He instinctively breathed in her sweet strawberry scent and was sad when she pulled away. She looked at the group.

"You all behave. Show Mark a good first meal here and we'll all be happier for it. Okay?"

The group murmured in agreement and Babs walked away, laughing quietly.

At lunch and dinner, the group talked with each other as though they had been in the facility for years, rather than months or weeks. Mark was quickly able to assess that Jenny had, in fact, suffered brain damage when the military bus she had been driving was hit in the blowback from a car bomb. Her family was unable to care for her needs and she'd been placed in the facility for long-term care. She held her own, conversation-wise and would, at times, become completely coherent, as if there had never been a problem at all. Minutes later, she would revert to child-like thinking and behaviors. David, Victor and Bob were always nice to her, though they tended to put her on notice if she began to act too irrationally.

Mark liked them all.

He lay in bed that first night, thinking about their conversations. He smiled, remembering something humorous and sighed contentedly. Perhaps the facility wouldn't be so bad after all.

His eyes snapped open.

He sat up in bed. He'd heard a noise. He knew he did, even though it was dead silent. He listened closely, moving his eyes around the dark room, feeling almost blind. There was no light coming in through his window. The moon must be behind clouds. He focused on the night sky through the glass but couldn't spot even one star.

"What the hell is going on?" He thought.

He jumped when he heard the sound that had woken him ring out in the quiet once more. It was a gunshot. Definitely a gun shot. His heart sped up. He looked at his wheelchair, which was not where it was supposed to be. He liked to keep it right next to the bed, so that he could slide into it quickly. It was all the way across the room.

He heard a thump. He wondered why the sound had not happened immediately after the shot. He heard scratching sounds, as though something was being dragged across a wooden floor. His breath came and went rapidly. Chills covered his arms, running in waves up his spine, washing over his hammering heart.

He watched in stunned silence as the door to his room slowly opened, allowing light from the outer hallway to spill in. He watched as the back end of a man came through. He was dragging a body into the room. Mark could see bloody trails the dragged body was leaving behind on the floor.

He opened his mouth but could not speak. His door stayed open, letting in the light. Now he saw that the room was littered with bodies...at least three others besides the one the man was dragging in.

Rage filled him, extinguishing his confusion and concern. He wanted to leap out of the bed, grab the murderer and snap his pathetic neck.

His hands balled up into fists and his jaw clenched. If he had superhuman powers, if he only had the use of his legs...

The man turned and stared directly at him, causing him to freeze in place. The man was dressed in the green uniform of the Vietnam war era. Mark instantly knew who he was. The symbol on the side of this shirt indicated he was a Sergeant. Sgt. Hall approached until he was leaned over, his face mere inches from Mark's.

"I did my part, buddy," he grumbled in low voice. *"Now it's your turn."*

Chapter Five

Mark sat up in bed, suddenly awake. The sun was peeking in through the window. He looked around frantically but the room was empty other than him, no bodies on the floor, no blood trailing in through the door, no Vietnam vet trying to terrify him.

He could still see Sgt. Hall, his face so close to him, appearing so very real. He could hear the words he'd growled out. *"Now it's your turn."*

What could that mean? Mark's career of killing the enemy was over. He couldn't walk. He would be sent stateside to live a miserable, unhappy life alone until he finally died.

His wheelchair was next to his bed, as it was supposed to be. He pulled himself into it and settled in, trying to get comfortable. He grabbed a pillow from his bed and put it behind his back. Sighing, he went to the bathroom to brush his teeth and get ready for the day.

Everything in the bathroom was eye level for him. As soon as he entered the room, he felt cold and knew something was wrong. It only took a glance in the mirror to see what it was. His reflection was not his own. It was the face of Sergeant Jerry Hall. He pushed himself immediately back out of the room, rolling backwards so quickly he bumped into the bed. His breathing was loud and anxious. Was he still dreaming?

He looked around.

He couldn't be. It was too real. It *was* real.

You think you can rid of me that easy? He heard whispered into his ear. He turned sharply but no one was beside him. You can't see me, you fool. You are me. It's time to do what you know you have to do.

"Get out of my head!" Mark leaned forward, holding both fists up against the sides of his head. "Get out! Get out of my head!"

Beating yourself up isn't going to make me go away. Mark hated the sound of the ghostly voice, sweeping through his mind like hot steam.

You need to do this. These people are responsible for all the bad things that have happened to you in your life. They need to pay.

"That's insane! You're making me insane! You're going to make me look crazy to all these people. Get out of my head. Leave me alone!" He shoved his chair in the direction of the door. He wanted to leave the room immediately.

The chair made it to about two feet from the door before the wheels froze in place. He pushed on them as hard as he could but even with his muscles bulging, the wheels would no longer move.

He had been trained to fight an enemy...an enemy he could see. How was he supposed to fight one that he could not see, one that was embedded in his mind? His mind raced with memories that weren't his, he could see military authority figures in front of his eyes, yelling at him. He could feel the resentment Sgt. Hall let brew deep inside of him, welling up until the young man could no longer take it. He let out his anger in an explosive way, slaughtering the other four residents in the wing Mark was now staying.

If he had his way, Mark knew Sgt. Hall would take over his body. If that happened, everyone in the facility was in danger. But what could he do?

You aren't going out of this room. Not until you are ready to do what needs to be done.

"I will never do it." Mark spoke through clenched teeth. "I will never do what you want me to do. I will leave this room. I will get out and tell them..."

His mind whirled. What would he tell them? That a ghost was haunting him? That it would force him to do unspeakable things, slaughter not the enemy but the innocent?

He couldn't do that without putting himself in more trouble. They might restrain him. Keep him under constant supervision, no matter where he was or what he was doing.

You don't have a choice.

"If I do what you want, they will put me on death row. I do have a choice. I can either kill innocent people or sacrifice my life."

No one will sacrifice themselves for others. You aren't so noble so don't kid yourself.

"I'm not trying to be noble." Mark leaned forward and grabbed the pillow from behind his back. He threw it on the ground in front of him and shoved himself out of the chair. "I'm just not going to kill innocent people."

You joined the army so you could kill people.

"I joined so I could kill the enemy. Every enemy. No innocent." Mark pulled himself over the thin carpeting toward the door after landing safely on the pillow. He wasn't sure how strong he was, after more than six months of being confined to a wheelchair. He wasn't sure if his bones would break. He tried sliding the pillow along under him and was finding the entire thing incredibly difficult to do. He looked up at the doorknob. It looked a million miles away, even though it was lower than regular doorknobs.

He reached up to grasp the doorknob, pulling his torso up from the floor. He felt something solid press hard against his chest, slamming him back down to the ground. He tried again and again, but the force would not let him reach the doorknob.

I told you, the voice sent painful anger coursing through his body. *The only way you're going out there, buddy, is to do what you need to do.*

Chapter Six

Frustration and anger were mounting in his mind. Mark couldn't move. All he could think about was keeping the sergeant from possessing his body somehow. He wished he had some salt or something, anything that the many ghost and demon hunters he'd seen on TV used to get rid of ghosts. He could hear chuckling, which fueled his rage even more, like throwing lighter fluid on a burning fire.

Those people out there aren't innocent. They might not have done something to you directly but they are part of the reason you're stuck here.

"That's stupid. That's insane. You don't know what you're talking about." Mark had grown weary trying to open the door. He crawled back to his chair and pulled himself up in it. A plan was forming in his mind. He didn't know whether the ghost sergeant could hear his thoughts so he tried to think in a scattered manner, only letting himself glimpse the seed of the plan. He wanted to help it grow without the sergeant catching on to what he planned to do.

He rolled his chair to the bathroom once again and went in. His heart was pounding hard as he tried not to focus on Sgt. Hall in the mirror. He reached up and pulled on the mirror, hoping beyond hope it was a medicine cabinet. When it came open, he frantically searched the small shelves for what he wanted. Relief flooded him when he saw it. He reached up and pulled the straight razor down.

Looks like you're all ready to go.

"I'm not using this on those innocent people out there." He pictured the other members of his wing, Jenny with her child-like mind, David with the one eye, constantly doing Popeye impressions that were too on point for his own good, Victor with his thick accent and Bob with the one arm, proudly proclaiming he would never be held in handcuffs again. He knew they were good people. He suspected the people Sgt. Hall had killed were just as innocent.

No one is innocent, Sgt. Geer. You need to do what's right. You need to end their misery. They are just as unhappy as you are. They have been mutilated by this world. They need you to end it for them so they can go on to a better place.

"That's not my call. If God didn't want them here, they wouldn't be here."

You can't possibly believe that crap. Take the straight razor and do what's right for those people. You think you care about them? If you really did, you'd be following my call to action right now and we wouldn't be debating it.

"Nope. You aren't going to convince me." He left the bathroom and moved his chair in such a way that it bumped the side of his bed. When it did, he slipped his hand under the side railing that was used to help him get in and out of it. There was a small button on the side of the metal part of the bed. He pressed it once and let go, hoping once would be enough to summon a nurse or someone to his room.

He pulled the straight razor open and pressed the edge of it against his wrist.

Don't do that. He could tell Sgt. Hall was not happy to see what he was planning to do. He rested the edge of the blade there for a prolonged period of time, his heart thumping. Where was the nurse? Surely someone saw his signal. Thoughts buzzed through his mind. What if the light outside his room didn't turn on? What if there was no one at the nurse's desk or the receptionist desk? What if the doctor wasn't there that early in the morning?

What are you doing? Don't be so stupid!

"I figure if they find another vet has killed himself in this room, they will shut it off to more patients."

Don't be a martyr. They aren't worth it!

"They don't deserve to die. Not at my hand. I won't kill them."

To his utter relief, there was a quick knock on his door before it swung open and Babs put her head in. She already looked concerned but when her eyes dropped to the straight razor in his hand, she leapt into the room and grabbed him, pulling the razor away from his skin.

"What are you doing, Mark? What are you thinking? You can't do this!" She went on, berating him in a kind and concerned voice, folding the straight razor and sliding it into her pocket. She went from terror to confusion, staring down at him. He'd put up no fight.

"I will do it again if I'm not let out of this room." He said. He could hear Sgt. Hall cussing both of them out but straightened what was left of his spine, squaring his shoulders and looking defiant. "I refuse to stay in this room another minute."

Babs leaned forward, her voice gentle as she spoke. "All you had to do was ask for a transfer, Mark. You don't have to kill yourself to be moved."

He smiled at her. He pulled in a deep breath of sweet strawberry scent. He glanced over his shoulder with a sneer as Babs pushed his chair out of the room.

In the end, those in authority decided to move Mark to a completely different facility, where the other patients were not strictly military but were there for spinal injuries. Now everyone he was around was in a wheelchair. The men had formed a basketball team and spent a lot of time training each other how to do common things without letting the wheelchair hold them back.

He made several friends just on the first day, openly expressing his love for basketball, confessing he'd been sure he would never play another day in his life. His new friends let him know that was definitely not the case. He went to bed the first day feeling open, free and happy for the first time in nearly a year.

As he fell asleep, he felt a cool breeze blow over him.

His eyes snapped open.

He heard a faint, low chuckling drift through the air toward his ears.

Sorry, buddy, he heard. *I told you ya wouldn't get rid of me that easy. It's your turn to do what you need to do, sergeant. And this time, there's gonna be a lot more bodies to pile up.*

Mark squeezed his eyes shut, fighting instant rage, gripping the pillow under his head until his knuckles were white.

"No," he said. "No, no, no, no!"

www.ingramcontent.com/pod-product-compliance
Lightning Source LLC
Chambersburg PA
CBHW031410150726
47989CB00002B/591